W9-BDR-163

The Big Outfit

Also by Peter Dawson in Thorndike Large Print®

Gunsmoke Graze
Royal Gorge
High Country

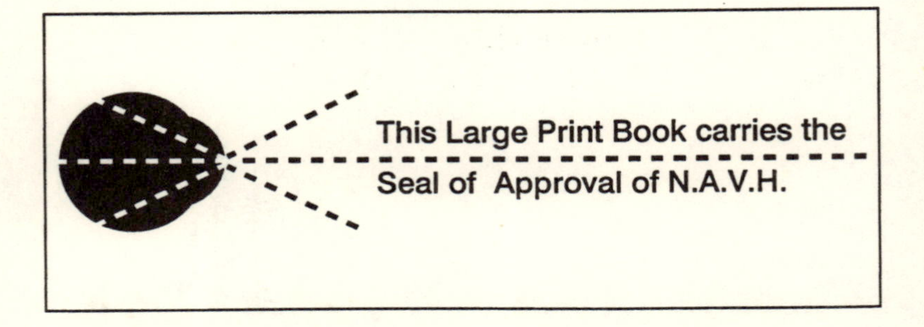

LP
F
D326

The Big Outfit

PETER DAWSON

Howard County Library
Big Spring, Texas 79720

Thorndike Press • Thorndike, Maine

Copyright © 1954 by Jonathan H. Glidden.
Copyright © 1955 by The Chicago Tribune Publishing Company.
Copyright © 1955 in the British Commonwealth. Renewed ® 1983
by the Estate of Jonathan Hurff Glidden.

All rights reserved.

Thorndike Large Print ® Western Series edition published in 1993
by arrangement with Golden West Literary Agency.

The tree indicium is a trademark of Thorndike Press.

Set in 16 pt. News Plantin by Juanita Macdonald.

This book is printed on acid-free, high opacity paper. ♾

Libary of Congress Cataloging in Publication Data

Dawson, Peter, 1907–
The big outfit / Peter Dawson.
p. cm.
ISBN 1-56054-698-0 (alk. paper : lg. print)
1. Large type books. I. Title.
[PS3507.A848B54 1993]
813′.54—dc20 93-7033
CIP

The characters, places, incidents and situations in this book are imaginary and have no relation to any person, place or actual happening.

Chapter 1

Darkness came early that first afternoon of the storm, with no let-up in the blistering cold or the wind and snow. At four-thirty, when Jim Harbour turned the team of blacks from the drifted ruts of the road, the light was so weak that memory as much as sight served him in reining on through the pines. And only the tilting of the wagon's seat shortly told him that he had found what he was looking for, a sheltered pocket in the timber where a high rock outcrop would offer him some protection for the night.

He swung stiffly down from the wagon and, wading through the drifts, finally found a windfall and broke some branches from it. His fire laid, he spent half a minute carefully paring shavings from a tallow candle, his long fingers stiff and awkward with the knife. The fire caught with the first match and he breathed a sigh of thankfulness at finding the wood was pitch.

Within five more minutes, he had unhitched the team and fed them, using grain-filled nosebags he pulled from beneath the carcass of a bull elk under the wagon's tarp. Only then did he carry a heavy grub-sack and a bedroll back to the fire, shake the snow from his wide hat, unbuckle his heavy wool coat and open it to the warmth of the blaze. Presently, when this past hour's bone-deep chill was gone from his tall and rangy frame he went back to the wagon for an axe.

In twenty more minutes he had cut and trimmed a dozen aspen poles and dragged them in to his camp, welcoming the warmth of the exertion. A pair of aspen saplings grew some twelve feet out from the granite wall in line with the fire and he roped their tops and tied them to a finger of rock so that their stems were bent well forward. He stacked the poles up along their trunks, lacing cuttings of oak brush between them. In the end he had a shoulder-high barrier that cut off the wind and the snow slanting in from the north and caught the heat of the blaze beginning to be reflected from the granite face of the outcrop.

All the while this big man had moved deliberately, almost lazily. Yet there had been no pausing, no motion wasted. And now as he sauntered out to the wagon once more, threw back its tarp and cut a front quarter from the carcass of a doe, his every move held that same sureness and economy of motion.

He had shouldered the meat and started back to the fire when suddenly he halted, having caught some subtle, stray hint of alien sound riding faintly in over the moaning of the wind.

He stood motionless, listening for several seconds. Then abruptly he eased his burden into the snow, stepped to the wagon. Hanging inside its improvised high splashboard were a Winchester and a double-barreled shotgun. It was the shotgun Harbour lifted from its pegs before he moved quickly in behind a nearby clump of oak.

Kneeling there, the shotgun resting against one knee, he shortly made out a shape drifting toward him from out of the blackness in the direction of the road.

In another moment he could see that it was a horse and buggy. Whoever this was pulled his animal to a stand just short of the wagon and sat staring toward the fire. Harbour waited a quarter-minute while the figure on the buggy's seat sat motionless. Then suddenly the newcomer was calling querulously.

"All right, you damned Indian. Get it over with."

Strong surprise washed out a degree of the tension holding Jim Harbour. He came slowly erect, wondering at this man being here. And there was little welcome in his voice as he answered, "Go on in, Gardies."

The newcomer's head swung sharply in Harbour's direction. He must have noticed the shotgun, for he said tonelessly, dryly, "You're a trusting soul," before bringing his horse past the wagon and in on the fire.

Following, Harbour came into the light to see the man in the buggy lift out a pair of crutches, throw back a laprobe and laboriously shift his bulk around on the seat. It was an awkward, painful thing to watch then as Gardies moved his useless legs over the side, leaned down and somehow managed to ease his weight onto the crutches and then aground without falling. Harbour could have helped, didn't.

Gardies was an old man with the craggy lines of his hawkish face softened by a greying spade beard. He wore a bulky buffalo coat that now made his movements ungainly as he swung slowly in on the fire and then watched Harbour lean the shotgun against the inside of the makeshift shelter. And when Harbour laid the quarter of venison in the snow near the fire, then knelt to draw his knife and begin slicing the meat, Gardies' expression took on a disdainful quality.

Jim Harbour knew his visitor barely well enough not to be surprised at the old man remaining silent. Curious as to why Gardies was here, as to how the storm could have caught him in this high country, an ingrained stubbornness nonetheless kept him from asking any question, in fact from saying anything. He set about getting his meal with no outward sign that he was aware of not being alone.

"Don't cut none of that for me." Gardies spoke suddenly, gruffly across the wind-restless silence.

"Who said it was for you?"

Harbour dropped a second steak into the skillet. There was a strong pride in him then, along with a bridled anger that made him think, *Keep him whittled down to your size.*

There was not a shred of friendliness between these two, and now Gardies let that be known by dryly stating, "A market hunter. Thought you'd given up selling meat now that you own a brand."

"Thanksgiving's three days from now," Harbour drawled, looking up at the man. "I'm doing this as a favor for some friends in town."

"How much meat you got stacked in that wagon?" When Harbour only shrugged, Gardies went on, "Quite a load. Getting money for it?"

"Game's about the only free thing in this country. The only thing that doesn't wear the

Gardies mark. Any reason why I shouldn't sell it?"

"Not any." Gardies appeared strangely unruffled at the barbed words, and added with a certain mildness, "If you manage to run the antelope on your way down tomorrow, knock over a couple for me. Take 'em to the church, say they're from me and that they're to be used to piece out the Thanksgiving supper. Nothing I hate worse than to have to eat turkey twice the same day. I'll pay you for the meat."

"The reverend was told two weeks ago he'd be getting meat to go with the turkey this year," Harbour said, adding pointedly, "Meat from me."

Gardies' face shaped a sudden and unexpected smile. "By God, you're all they say you are. Proddy. Won't back down to no one."

"Which, if true, makes us two of a kind."

The old man chuckled. "So it does." His manner then resumed its customary faint truculence as he announced, "I was up at your layout. First time I've laid eyes on it. You've taken too much care with things, built too good."

Harbour managed nicely to conceal his surprise at Gardies having visited his high country meadow. "Why too good?"

"Because the winters up here'll drive you out in the end."

"It won't be a winter that drives me out," Harbour said with unmistakable meaning. "You ought to know what a choice spot it is with all that wild hay. My cattle will winter better than yours down below."

The old man considered this over a deliberate interval, finally musing, "To think I let you take it from me."

"It was never yours to be taken away. It was open . . ."

A lift of Gardies' hand cut Harbour short. The old man shifted his weight on the crutches. "We won't argue the point. You saw a thing you wanted, you took it and hung on. It's legally yours even if you did have to shoot up a crew of men —"

"One man, not a crew."

"One man who'll never forget. And two of his crew were with him. Evan Rue's got a memory longer than mine even. One day you'll discover that."

Gardies' glance took on a smug quality. "Just for the tally book, tell me something. Was it accident or skill that let you shoot that gun out of Rue's hand and leave him with his stiff finger?"

Jim Harbour debated an answer, finally saying, "You've got more of a reason for be-

[illegible] here than to make this kind of small t[illegible]

[illegible]ld man smiled crookedly. "Just wonder[illegible]at you'd say," he grunted. "You see, I know."

Harbour frowned. "What do you know?"

"Where you came from three years ago."

A wariness and a slow anger were gripping Harbour then as Gardies went on, "It took a long time and it cost me some money. I paid a man to track you down. You're not only a market hunter but you've been a man hunter." He saw Harbour stiffen and was pleased. "One hell of a good one, so they say. What made you turn in your badge and come three hundred miles to hide yourself in this neck of the woods?"

Harbour's voice was toneless, cool as he drawled, "You have a reputation for not wasting words. You're wasting them now. Get it said, whatever reason you've got for being here."

Raoul Gardies' glance wavered now, fell away, and for a pronounced interval he stared at the fire as though watching the flakes of snow swirling down into the flames. Finally he eyed Harbour once more, saying quietly, "Phillip three nights ago lost his Cow Springs layout to Evan Rue in a game of draw at Wickwire's place."

His solemn words caught Jim Harbour in the act of reaching down for a length of wood to feed the fire. Harbour's hand went motionless, he looked up at Gardies in [illegible]ight disbelief. "Phil what?"

"You heard." Gardies watched him straighten, watched the astonishment go out of his blue eyes and anger replace it. Only then did he say, "Soon as I heard about it I sent Neal in to check. The game was fair and square. Phil had been losing and couldn't borrow to cover a four hundred dollar raise of Rue's. He had a good hand. So he put up title to the Springs quarter-section to cover the raise."

Jim Harbour tossed the length of pine onto the blaze now, staring vacantly at the shower of sparks that swirled upward. He was confused, his thinking revolving around the meaning of all this. "Couldn't Phil still put up the money instead?"

"Where would he get the four hundred?"

"From his father."

The old man laughed bitterly. "Think he'd ask me for it? Think Rue would take it?" . . . He shook his head, sighing gustily . . . "Look at Phil. Look at the way he drinks and gambles. Look at that woman he was chasing before she left for Laramie last month."

"There was nothing so bad about Ruth Jones."

"She sang in the *Niagara*, Harbour, not in church."

"Since when have you taken to wearing the cloak of a deacon?" There was a rough edge of scorn to Harbour's voice as he showed his dislike for this man. "Don't they say you were living with a Blackfoot squaw when you were Phil's age? Don't they —"

"Those were different times," Gardies interrupted heatedly. He paused then on the point of defending himself further, saying almost mildly, "Once again, we won't argue the point. A better point is that Phil's given Rue the chance he's been waiting for. Handed it to him on a silver platter. Which puts me in a tight spot."

"You in a tight spot?" Harbour laughed mockingly. "You lose a quarter section 'way off at the east edge of your range. Which leaves you with maybe only two hundred square miles of grass."

"You know what this means as well as I do," the old man countered patiently, even gently. "It's not the amount of land that counts. What does count is that Rue will try and join up Crow Track and the Springs by moving onto all that graze between the two."

Jim Harbour had had this thought a minute

ago, at Gardies' first mention of his son's lost gamble. Yet he nevertheless drawled, "Let the pack jump you and tear Bit apart. I'll shed no tears after what you did to me."

"Won't you now?" Gardies' look was smug, secretive. "Look at the way your neck of the hills sticks out across that graze Rue's got his eye on. Son, you're in trouble."

"If I am I'll take care of it. If Rue pushes cattle up near me, they get pushed right back down."

"Do they?" Tightening his grip on the crutches, Gardies leaned forward. "Spring before last when you made Rue back down to you he had a two man crew. He was still the saddle tramp I kept back off the bench fifteen years ago when he tried to settle on my range. He —"

"Range you claim but don't own."

Raoul Gardies tossed his head, scorning the remark. "It's mine till someone can push me off. Always has been and always will be," he stated. "But we're straying from the point. Which is that now Rue has a following among that pack up north. And last summer's election put his one armed hero friend into the sheriff's office. They've been waiting for their chance at me. This gives it to them."

He lifted his hands outward, letting his weight sag onto the crutches as he looked down at his useless legs. "Look at me. So damn' crippled I can't put one foot ahead of the other. If I was in shape to ride I'd jump Rue the first move he makes onto that middle grass."

"Don't expect me to be sorry for you," Harbour drawled. "You're an old man. You've had your day and you've brought plenty of misery to other people, me included. No one's going to hate it much if you have your troubles now. So why come up here to cry on my shoulder? All this is between you and Rue."

"Is it?" the old man flared. "Come off the prod, man. You've got the brains to see you're wound up in this just as tight as I am."

"I've already said I'll handle my end of it."

With a sudden and impatient squaring of his shoulders, Gardies said, "Let's talk no more hogwash, Harbour. I came here to do you a favor. One in which I'll be doing myself a favor, too."

"Naturally."

Raoul Gardies overlooked the jibe, continuing, "I've got a good bunch of men on my payroll. Only eleven now with the winter lay-off, but all good. I need a man with the guts to rod that crew if trouble comes. You're that man."

Shock and disbelief of what he was hearing

were strong in Jim Harbour one moment. The next he was struck by the utter incongruity of what Gardies had said. He couldn't repress a chuckle. It prolonged itself into loud, gusty laughter.

The Bit owner's expression didn't change. "Get that out of your system, then think it over carefully," he growled. "I've got brains or I wouldn't be where I am today. I've thought this out. You're the only man in twenty years who's ever taken anything from me and made it stick. If you've got the guts to do that, you should be working for me. You're the only man I know who can do what I want done."

Harbour shook his head in bafflement, still smiling. "You've got Neal. He's had practice kicking people around for Bit. What's wrong with him?"

"Neal knows cattle and he can run a good bluff. But he's not the man to send against a bunch of real hard cases. His job's the only thing he'd have at stake in this. You'd have more at stake than just the job."

"I'll look after my own stake, not yours. The hell with you, Gardies."

The old man's face flushed, yet he kept a tight rein on his temper. "I'll let you put two or three men up at your place to watch it. They'll do the chores and it won't cost you a dollar. You can name your own pay."

"No. Find someone else." Harbour had a thought then that made him add, "Give Phil a try at it."

Raoul Gardies laughed harshly, his voice rasping across the sound of the wind restlessly moaning through the tops of the pines. "The boy's soft. Not worth a quarter of what his sister is." His glance narrowed and he said, "You don't know Renee, but she's got what Phil lacks. She's coming home tomorrow. From three years of being with my relatives in France, in Paris."

Harbour had nothing to say and the old man went on, "I want to do this for her. If she was a man I'd have no problem."

"If you had friends, any friends at all, you'd have no problem."

Raoul Gardies' eyes brightened in anger. But he held that in check once again, saying levelly, "I want you to think this over, sleep on it. The offer's still good whenever you change your mind."

"I won't change it."

Gardies turned clumsily now and swung in half a dozen strides of his crutches across to the buggy. Once again Harbour witnessed a painful procedure as the man first sat on the floor of the buggy and then used the strength of his powerful shoulders and arms to pull himself up onto the seat.

As he unwound the reins from the whip socket, he looked across at Harbour to say dourly, "Thanks for the help."

"Wasn't any trouble at all," Harbour said.

Gardies pulled his animal around and drove away into the dark smother of the storm without another word. And Harbour, suddenly ravenous, squatted by the fire, took out his knife and began cutting one of the steaks.

Jim Harbour left his blankets an hour before dawn the following morning, built up his fire and then hitched and fed the mare and gelding. By the time he had finished breakfast and loaded grub-sack and bedroll into the wagon, a faint grey light was thinning the blackness over the Arrowheads.

It was still snowing fitfully. Though the wind had died, he found open stretches along the road badly drifted. He drove for the better part of an hour after breaking camp, toward the end of that interval passing a fork that led to his homestead meadow three miles away across the hills.

For a time he thought back upon his talk with Raoul Gardies last night, still feeling a strong measure of surprise and amusement at the old man's offer, along with a certain satisfaction over the way they had parted. Being still of the same mind as he had been then, he thought of Evan Rue more in relation to himself than to Bit, and those thoughts were sobering.

The strengthening light of the tardy dawn found him slowly and carefully working his way through a cat-tail thicket edging the unfrozen inlet at the head of Mirror Lake. The steady fall of snow surrounded him with a whispering rustle as the big flakes settled against the dried stalks. Shortly he was within two strides of the lake's margin and peering through the last screening cat-tails to see duck and geese rafted across the open water, some of the birds scarcely ten yards away.

Harbour felt a strong compunction about this kind of shooting. Yet because he had Thanksgiving orders for a dozen or so duck and geese, he slowly brought the Greener to shoulder and carefully took aim, knowing that this would probably be his one chance of getting any number of birds.

After his two deliberate shots he reloaded quickly and stayed in position. He was lucky enough to have a small wedge of mallard, along with three geese, swing back and circle low overhead. And this time he spent his two shells on wing shots, bringing down two of the geese. Afterward he waded the shallows to collect his bag, then made two trips on out to the wagon, his long stride awkward because of the heavy gum boots he wore, the deep snow and the weight he carried.

In twenty more minutes, taking the wagon down the road toward the pass, he came upon turkey and shot a tom and two hens before the flock panicked and soared down and away through the aspen and lodgepoles. His luck held even after that. As the C & W's big snowshed at the top of the pass came hazily into view a short time later, a buck bounded suddenly from an oak thicket ahead.

Harbour snatched up the Winchester and brought the animal down in a cartwheeling fall at precisely the instant it was disappearing over a ridge crest nearly a hundred yards away. Nine out of ten men would have taken considerable pride in such a shot, yet Harbour carefully examined the rifle's sights once he discovered that his bullet had hit behind the shoulder rather than at the base of the neck as he had intended it should.

The dressing out and the loading of the deer took him a scant five minutes, for he had performed this chore countless times. Then shortly, going on toward the line of the narrow gauge's drifted embankment and widely spaced telegraph poles, he was surprised at the sight of smoke clouding the near end of the long timbered structure that served as a refuge for this remote spur's stormbound trains.

Knowing that the snow wasn't yet deep enough to have stalled a train, he presently gave way to a strong curiosity and turned his animals from the road and across there. He was some sixty yards short of the snowshed's high open maw when the thinning haze of falling snow let him see the flicker of a small fire and the outline of a figure standing by it.

He pulled the team to a stand close below the end of the shed and looked up at a girl who held a rich bottle-green cape gathered tightly about her slender waist. He lifted a hand to touch the brim of his hat. "Not much of a day to be out seeing the sights, miss."

"Hardly."

Smiling, she came around the fire now and stood at the embankment's edge, looking down at him. And for a moment he sat startled, held speechless by her striking looks. Never had he seen a face molded in such perfection, nor one so expressive and alive as this girl's. That face was framed by the cape's fur-lined hood, and by hair so dark that even in this poor light it bore the sheen of a blackbird's wing.

The girl's cheeks were glowing with the stinging cold, and now as her green eyes appraised Harbour with an open, friendly interest, she told him, "Ben Britt wrecked his stage half a mile below. I was his only passenger, so he's gone to town to get a rig and take me the rest of the way to Bit." As an afterthought she added, "I'm Renee Gardies."

A definite reserve settled through Jim Harbour, though he said politely, "Jim Harbour. I live up above." He had no wish to carry the conversation further, though he knew that common courtesy demanded that he should, and asked, "How long have you been here?"

"Since about five o'clock. The stage was late because of the storm."

He sensed from her sobering manner that she had been quick to catch his reaction to the mention of her name. And now he tried to sound more affable as he queried, "Ben had been hitting the jug?"

"Doesn't he always?" She laughed, apparently relieved at finding him less reserved than a moment ago.

The spontaneity of her good humor was infectious, and he smiled broadly. But then the next moment he was serious again, "Ben'll be half the day getting back. I'm headed for town. I could take you on home."

"But that would be taking you four miles

out of your way. Or eight altogether."

He shrugged. "I'm in no hurry."

"Really?" She was plainly relieved. "Then I'd be very grateful."

She came down the embankment and he stepped aground to help her up onto the seat. And as he walked around and climbed up beside her, she told him, "I appreciate this. Having to just stand and wait this close to home is like . . . well, like being hungry and not being able to eat the things you see in a store window."

Wonder if she's ever been really hungry? Harbour was immediately ashamed of the pettiness of the thought, and of the rancor that had prompted it. To cover his disquieting feeling that this Gardies might just possibly be different from the two others, her father and brother, he asked, "Could I get your things from the stage?"

"No. I can send somebody for them."

He lifted a heavy buffalo robe from the wagon's bed and shook the snow from it before laying it across her lap. Then, as he put the gelding and the mare into motion, swinging them back toward the road, she told him, "I saw you bring down that buck. It was a fine shot."

"A lucky one."

Harbour was suddenly and contrarily

thinking back upon last night's conversation with Raoul Gardies, and once again the strong antagonism he felt toward Bit rose in him. He had never been to the ranch. He doubted that anyone but the girl would greet his appearance there this morning with anything but a grudging tolerance. And it was this thought that made him respond to Renee Gardies' attempts at making conversation now with brief, sometimes monosyllabic answers as they took the winding road down off the pass.

The timber sheltered them from the wind for the first three miles below the train shed. Harbour held his animals to a steady trot, wanting only to get the drive over with. The girl was quick to respect his indrawn mood and spoke only twice, briefly, over the final two miles that put them within sight of the bench's hazed and unbroken sweep at the foot of the hills.

At that point he became hard aware of the fact that he had made his feelings too obvious. He began trying to think of something to say to break the strained silence, at length looking around at her and asking awkwardly, "Warm enough?"

"Yes, thank you."

There was little warmth in either her tone or the glance her green eyes gave him, and he told himself, *Forget her.* But he had long ago found he couldn't put aside his strong awareness of this girl. The swaying of the wagon would occasionally bring her shoulder against his, and he was very conscious of a scent she wore, one as light and fresh as this mountain air.

Quite suddenly she was saying, "I suppose this is just a sample of what I'll be getting from now on."

He was startled, puzzled, and when he glanced at her it was to find her striking face set in complete soberness. "A sample of what?"

"Of dislike. Of mistrust."

Jim Harbour could feel the blood mounting to his face. Caught completely by surprise, wishing he could be any place but here beside this outspoken girl, his first instinct was to pretend ignorance of what she was talking about.

But then a rebellion rose in him against giving in to her, or to any Gardies, and he asked, "Would you expect it to be any other way?"

"At least you're honest enough not to deny it." Over a brief pause, she told him, "It's just occurred to me who you are. Phil has written about you."

Halfway sensing where her words were leading, he said patiently, "Look, miss, suppose we get you home without a wrangle. You know and I know that no amount of talk will settle anything."

"But I intend that it shall settle something."

He breathed a long sigh, tilting his head as a gust drove a fine spray of snow at them, afterward asking, "Just what?"

"You're going to understand something about Bit, about my father."

"I understand enough already. Too much maybe."

In seeming irrelevance, she asked, "You know why dad's let you stay up here, don't you?"

"Suppose you tell me."

"It's because of the way you handled Evan Rue. Was it a year ago, or two? Anyway, according to Phil dad thinks you're worth having around if Rue's afraid of you."

"I doubt that he is."

She considered this and finally shrugged in an uncaring way. "Why is it that you all hate us so? You, Rue, everyone."

Harbour was ordinarily a man of few words. But now a contrary impulse made him drawl, "All right, if you want to listen here are my reasons. When I first came to this country the courthouse books all said this was open range. So I filed on a quarter section. Then —"

"Anyone could have told you that Bit and Crow Track have used these hills as summer range for at least fifteen years."

"They could've, but they didn't. Maybe they thought they'd play me for a sucker and could watch some fun. Anyway, I filed and came up. Spent the first winter cutting logs, living in a brush wickiup, taking meat down to town every so often to sell it and help pay for things. That next spring your friend Rue brought —"

"Don't call Evan Rue my friend," she bridled.

"Anyway," he continued patiently, "I was lucky. When Rue ordered me to clear out, I bluffed him and his *compadres* into thinking it might pay them to let me alone. But in another month I began wondering how lucky I really was. When I went down to town to buy hardware and salt and a few other things, no one would do business with me. Wouldn't sell me so much as a ten-penny nail. Because your father had let it get around I wasn't wanted."

She said soberly, "Go on."

"There's not much more. I drove the twenty miles across the pass to Bend to buy what I needed. Then when it came time to stock the place last summer the same thing happened. No one around here would sell me even a fevered calf. So I bought from an outfit over near Lake City. Finally, just lately, a few stores in town have begun giving me credit. On the quiet, so your father won't get wind of it."

"Why did you stay?"

Harbour deliberated his answer. Knowing that sooner or later she would probably learn about his past from her father, he finally told her, "Maybe it was bullheadedness. Anyway, I'd saved a long time for this, for a place to call my own. I'd given up the no good job of wearing a law badge and ordering other people around. When it came to me being ordered around by Rue, it didn't take. Running the way these other settlers do when Bit cracks the whip gets a man into the habit of running from anything. So I stayed."

She was considering what he had said and presently asked, "You weren't in trouble when you came here? You weren't already running from something?"

He shook his head. "Only from my conscience." Bleakly, he added, "I'd had to put a man in his grave. He was a killer and he belonged in a box. But it seemed I wasn't the man to keep on earning wages at that trade. So I left it."

"All right, I can see your side of it," she said. "But I can see dad's side, too. None of these people you say Bit kicks around seem to realize that he was the first white man on the bench. That he persuaded the first lot of settlers to stay here and begin building the town. None of you give him credit for seeing that a post office and bank were opened. And for keeping the bank open with his money when poor times hit us. It's because of him that the railroad brought this branch line in. There are half a hundred things he's done for this country."

He carefully thought out his argument, at length drawling, "He did build up the country. But why didn't he let it grow? Why does Bit chouse the nesters and homesteaders off to the west of Owl Creek every spring? Why would your father make it so tough for me? I'm fourteen, fifteen miles from —"

"Because of what I said a minute ago," she cut in. "Because you're on our summer range. As for Owl Creek, it's our west boundary. You seem to forget, Harbour. You forget that dad trapped these mountains and shot buffalo here on the bench long before other white men had seen it. He was entitled to as much as he wanted of it."

"Times have changed."

"They have. With the range being eaten away, Bit's being crowded. Dad has to protect himself. Nothing could persuade him to change his mind on that."

Harbour smiled wryly. "He's already been persuaded, miss. That horse persuaded him."

Renee Gardies sensed the ungiving quality in this man and chose to ignore it now. "He'll never be able to walk again, will he?" she asked gently.

He lifted his wide shoulders in a spare shrug, flicking the reins to put his animals on faster along the levelling stretch of road ahead. "He gets around on crutches. Not well, but a little. They say his legs are gone. That horse fell down a slope with him, square onto him. He's lucky to be alive."

"And his heart's gone back on him, Phil writes." The girl gave him a proud angry look. "I suppose people are gloating over what happened, you among them."

Jim Harbour was weary of this pointless argument, of the bitterness that lay between them, and told her, "This isn't getting us anywhere. Let's forget it."

She eyed him aloofly, speculatively a moment. "I don't intend to forget it. Three years ago I tried to. By going away, using a visit to aunts and cousins in France as an excuse. I even thought I might stay away because I realized how it was here, because I'd argued with dad about it. I tried to like Paris. They taught me the language, taught me manners and how to wear fine clothes. I could even have married a man with a title."

Renee Gardies was staring at him intently as she went on, "Yet none of it mattered when I heard what had happened to my father. I had to come back. And," she concluded deliberately, "I don't intend to come back and see things go on as they were going when I left."

He laughed softly, reaching up to shake the snow from the back of his coat collar, "You'll probably find them worse than when you left. Rue and his bunch are beginning to feel their oats."

"Then I'll see that there's a change."

"How? By hirin' the church and preaching the gospel about what a fine outfit Bit is? On what a kind and generous soul Raoul Gardies is?" He thought of something, knowing it was unfair to mention it, his irritation nevertheless making him say, "Or will you admit to the congregation that he's so mean he's even driven his son from under his roof and made the makin's of a tramp of him?"

Her hand moved fast as a gunfighter's, lifting and catching him hard and full across the cheek, rocking his head around. The whole side of his face was smarting, stinging as he looked at her.

He was strangely without anger, hardly

even annoyed. Perhaps it was in thankfulness at having things so clearly understood between them that he drawled mildly, "Guess I had that coming to me."

She suddenly reached across to snatch the reins and haul back on them so sharply that the gelding started to rear. The wagon lurched to a stop. Turning from Harbour, lifting her skirt and stepping down to the wheel hub, she said tonelessly, "It can't be over half a mile to Murchison's place."

He made no attempt to stop her, only asked, "Do I send Murchison back after you?"

"You do not. I'm perfectly able to walk."

She was indignant, her green eyes blazed with a look of outrage and loathing. He avoided her glance, looking down at her shoes, at the snow almost covering their buttoned tops. "You'll freeze if you walk very far."

"I won't freeze and I am walking," she said brittlely. "Move on."

Harbour flicked the reins and put the wagon on down the road. He didn't look back.

George Wickwire had long ago given up trying to guess what effect bad weather had on his business. This raw and gloomy afternoon, with more snow falling steadily on top of the eight or ten inches already blanketing the town, the *Niagara* was as busy as on most weekday evenings. Two poker layouts were crowded, with again as many men watching the play, an even dozen customers idled at the bar and half that number were keeping the colored cook busy at the free food counter at the back end of the bar.

It was one of those unpredictable days that thinned Wickwire's skepticism on the wisdom of having bought the saloon from its ageing owner a year ago. He had come to Alder four winters ago and hired on as a gambler. He'd had no responsibilities beyond looking out for himself in any game of chance a customer wanted to name. This involved the minor annoyances of handling belligerent drunks, of taking so much but not too much abuse from the rare individual who wrongly suspected him of manipulating cards, of looking after the house's take and finally of judging when to press and when to ease away from a strong run of luck.

Now all that was changed. He had become a man burdened with heavy responsibilities and certain obligations, one of which he was at the moment engaged in fulfilling as he sauntered from his office and across to the rear poker layout to tap one of the players on the shoulder. He startled the man, who looked quietly up at him, then down at his outstretched hand.

"Today's pay day, Mart," the gambler stated quietly. "Let's have it."

The man started to reach to a pocket, then hesitated. "Now look, George. I'm in fine shape." . . . He gestured toward three high stacks of chips alongside his half-empty glass . . . "Must be twenty ahead. I promise —"

"Give."

One of the other players laughed dryly. "You asked him to, Mart. Better hand it across."

Grudgingly, the man took a buckskin money-sack from pocket, untied the draw-string and shook out a handful of silver dollars. He gave the largest portion of them to Wickwire. Counting the money, the saloon-man drawled, "You're three short," and held out his hand again.

He was given the three dollars and turned from the table as his victim took the guying of two or three of his companions. Wickwire crossed to the bar and handed the money to the apron, telling him, "This goes to the bank in the morning, Sid. In Lily's name."

A customer standing nearby said affably, "Let me buy you a drink, George," but Wick-wire shook his head and made his way to the front of the room to stand at the broad window looking out across the awninged walk and the snow-hazed street.

George Wickwire was a slender, soft-spoken man of medium height in his thirty-third year. Raised in a kindlier clime than this, a man who enjoyed his creature comforts, the blustery and chill look of the street made him shiver slightly and start turning from the window. But abruptly he paused, closely regarding a team and wagon approaching from the street intersection below.

In another moment he was sure it was Jim Harbour who sat the wagon's seat, and returned to the door, opened it and went out onto the walk. He stood shivering at the edge of the planks, coat collar turned up and hands in pockets as Harbour drew within hailing distance.

"Where to, Jim?"

Harbour looked this way, not answering but turning the blacks obliquely in toward the tie rail. Wickwire's discomfort and impatience made him call once more, "Want to see you," and then hurry back into the saloon.

He stood waiting by the door, looking through its upper glass half as Harbour got down and tied his team, then came across the walk beating the snow from the shoulders of his coat and stamping his boots. And as the door opened on him, the gambler said, "You sure pick your days. Why be out in this?"

"Had some orders for game."

"Better come on back and take something to ward off frostbite."

The gambler led the way along the bar, Harbour speaking or nodding to several of the customers as he followed. The office door had no sooner closed behind them than Wickwire went to a cabinet behind his desk, opened it and took a slender-necked decanter and two large shot-glasses from one of the shelves. He filled both glasses, offering one to Harbour. "Here's to a short, mild winter."

"Amen."

They emptied their glasses and set them on the desk, Harbour coughing and his eyes watering. "You'd think it was that liniment I sell out front," Wickwire drawled in mild reproof, checking his reach for the decanter as Harbour quickly said, "Easy, man. I've got a twelve mile drive back home."

Harbour took a pouch of tobacco from the pocket of his coat and was sifting some of the weed onto a wheat-straw paper when Wickwire asked, "How long since you were in, Jim?"

"Ten days or so."

"Hear about Phil Gardies getting a lesson in how to play draw the other night?"

Harbour looked up, nodding. When he had

nothing to say, the gambler asked, "Worried?"

"Should I be?"

"I wonder." Wickwire stepped around to sit in the swivel chair and lift his high-polished boots to the desk top. "In your place I should be . . . well, say uneasy."

Jim Harbour turned to the stove in the corner of the room and leaned down, holding his cigarette against the stove's lid and drawing on it until it was burning. As he straightened, he said, "George, my hair'd be white by now if I spent time thinking of all the things that could've happened these past three years."

"So it would. But this is different and you know it."

"Different how?"

"Friend Rue has been playing a waiting game. I should judge his waiting is about finished." Frowning, the gambler asked, "Ever sit with the man in a game of cards?"

"No. Would it prove anything if I had?"

"Probably not. You'd have had to watch him as I have over say twenty or thirty evenings. By then you'd know him."

Harbour smiled wryly. "Some read tea leaves, you go by the cards, eh?"

Wickwire nodded. "The man has an unholy amount of patience. Bides his time. When his luck comes along he crowds it to the limit. Phil Gardies learned that the other night."

Jim Harbour had been halfway amused. But now he matched the other's seriousness. "You're trying to tell me something, George. What is it?"

"I've already said it."

"That Rue plays 'em close to the belt? That I'm to watch him because he's got me sandwiched in between Crow Track and the Springs?"

"Exactly. Add a touch of seasoning to the sandwich. Which would be Bill Parks, our illustrious sheriff with the one arm. He and Rue fought the War together seventeen years ago. He'll back any play Rue makes."

It was impossible for Harbour to divorce what he was hearing now from what he heard from Raoul Gardies last night. And because of this there was a strong irritation in his tone as he asked, "What more's a man to do beyond keeping an eye open? If Rue crowds me, then's the time to buck him."

"You're wrong. Wrong as can be, Jim." The saloonman reached over to turn down the smoking wick of the lamp on his desk. "Rue's got as much right running cattle in those hills as you have. Except on your land. And if he does, you're licked. You've got how big a herd now? Sixty head, a hundred? You cut hay off how much land to carry that many? A section?"

"Just about."

"And you're proving upon only a quarter section. You know and I know that Rue's got as much legal right as you to that grass up there. So if he moves in, how's your herd to grow?"

He caught the anger brightening Jim Harbour's blue eyes and lifted a hand to check the outburst he saw coming. "We could talk ourselves black in the face and never settle the matter. After all, it's up to Rue and no one can tell for sure exactly what he'll try. Or when he'll try it. But you can out-guess him."

Pausing, smiling crookedly, he said, "Listen to me preach. Ready with all sorts of free advice."

"So far you haven't given any, free or otherwise."

"Want me to?"

Harbour nodded, sensing that the gambler was deadly serious despite the smile. And a moment later George Wickwire took his boots from the desk and leaned forward to ask, "Ever heard of land warrants, Jim? Land scrip?"

It took Harbour a long moment to nod in answer, "Didn't they give it to men who fought in the War?"

"No. They gave it to soldiers who served before the war. That's one kind of land warrant. There have been others, railroad scrip for one. Then the Sioux and the Chippewas were given another kind. But do you know how these warrants can be used?"

"To buy land with."

Wickwire nodded. "Either to buy outright or to use for homestead. A man can get patent on any open federal land with it. One section, five, or even fifty if he's got the warrants to cover that much."

"If he's got them," Harbour drawled.

The gambler turned and, nodding to indicate the safe in the room's near corner, said, "I've got them. I started picking scrip up four, five years ago purely as a speculation. Today you can buy it in most large towns through land brokers. Three months ago I bought some in Denver. I'd be willing to let you have some, sell it to you."

Harbour was surprised and his look showed it as the saloonman continued, "Use it to patent land around you. Say two sections, more if you want. Then let Rue do any damned thing he wants to long as he stays clear of you. If he doesn't keep clear, then get the law after him. Federal law."

Jim Harbour was taken aback by the unexpectedness and generosity of the offer. He couldn't guess what lay behind it, for he and this man were little more than good acquaintances. His only dealings with Wickwire had been in selling him game for the *Niagara*'s free meal counter. Occasionally, on his infrequent visits to the saloon, they would spend some time in talk. But they had never been close or known each other well.

Because of his strong puzzlement, he now said, "That's a mighty fine thing to offer a man and you've got my thanks. But I'm caught short. Almost every dollar to my name has gone into the layout. I couldn't put up the money to cover the warrants on even another quarter-section."

"I know that. You'd sign a note and pay me interest until you could pay off the full amount. We'd set a figure agreeable to both of us. I've bought most of this cheap. I've even taken some for gambling debts at a heavy discount. For most trading they usually figure warrants are worth a dollar and a quarter an acre. Mine has come anywhere between eighty cents and a dollar and a half. You could buy from me at a dollar thirty-five, which would be a good price for you and still make me a little."

Harbour frowned, asking, "Suppose you didn't get even your interest? Suppose —"

"Look, Jim. I take chances every day. I'll take one on you. If you couldn't meet interest payments, we'd work it out some way. You could start bringing me meat again, say. But these warrants aren't earning me a plugged nickel so long as they lie here in my safe."

He eased back in the chair again, musing, "Maybe you wonder why I'd like to see you make this kind of a bet. It's simply because I'm a contrary devil. Contrary enough to like Phil Gardies about as much as I dislike Rue, which is plenty. I'd like to lay some money on the hole card in this game."

"Meaning me?"

"You'll do until another hole card's dealt."

Harbour gave a slow shake of the head, at length saying, "Can't see taking the risk, George. You're talking to the tune of a thousand dollars even if I bought only enough warrants to get patent on a section. If it was a year from now and if I'd make some money on beef I'd take you up. As it is, I'm barely in the clear. It feels good. I'll keep it that way."

"It'd feel even better if you owned more of those hills around you."

Shrugging, Harbour turned to the door now. "Thanks anyway."

"Think it over, Jim. The offer stands tomorrow or the next day. Or six months from now."

* * *

The man on the dun gelding followed the heavy timber of the ridge until he was directly above the sideless barn. Reining in, he eased the weight of his squat, powerful body into one stirrup and, folding his arms and leaning against the horn, warily scanned the meadow below.

A light, powdery fall of snow obscured the hills to the south, yet even in this fading light he could clearly see the cattle bunched around the hay-stack near the trees off there at half a mile's distance, and the drifted line of the road leading out to the pass. The light was flat, there were no shadows, and it took him several seconds to decide that no fresh wheel tracks showed along the road. Finally certain of that, he shifted his glance downward to Jim Harbour's cabin.

No smoke came from the chimney, no light showed at the two windows within his vision. The corral flanking the barn was empty, its gates open. The place had the look of being deserted and he felt the urge to go down there at once, yet crowded it back. It would be dark in a few minutes. He wasn't taking any chances, not any.

A quarter-hour later, with the grey darkness thickening about him, he put the dun down the steep slope. As an afterthought he reached inside his coat and lifted a .45 Colt's from holster. He pulled the mitten from his right hand and thrust his bare hand holding the gun deep in coat pocket.

When he reached the level ground between barn and cabin he brought the dun to a stand and sat a moment listening, looking, feeling his pulse quicken. When it occurred to him that he was a little afraid he breathed a gusty, derisive "Ah-h-h!" and put his animal straight on across toward the cabin. He circled the building, pausing once to stare off into the thickening darkness across the meadow. Then, quickly, he rode to the door, came down out of the saddle and tried the latch.

The door refused to open. He put his shoulder against it and found it firmly secured. He stepped back a pace and lifted a boot, then checked himself, thinking of the noise he would make in kicking the door in. He thought of breaking a window, but that would also mean noise.

He was nervous, not at all liking this, and finally muttered, "The hell with it," and led the dun to the corner of the cabin nearest the barn, to an open fronted lean-to formed by two board walls running from the ground to the roof's wide overhang. Axed lengths of wood were neatly stacked from ground to roof against the cabin's logs. A mound of corncobs lay against one side wall. And near it was a stoneware jug.

Reaching for the jug, he pulled its cob stopper and put it to his nose. A broad, relieved smile patterned his face as he caught the rank odor of coal-oil. The smile held as he upended the jug and quickly sloshed the liquid onto the cobs.

Some moments later his hand had gone under his coat to a pocket of his shirt when a muffled sound shuttled in from the direction of the lower meadow. His eyes came wide open in alarm, and his hand was shaking as he brought out a match and hastily scratched it alight against the rough wall boards.

He dropped the match onto the corncobs. A lazy tongue of flame curled up, wiping away the darkness. He wheeled quickly and stepped over to the dun. Suddenly the flame spread, bathing him in a strong light. And now, with boot lifted to stirrup, he was hearing the jingle of doubletree chains sounding from the meadow. With a panicked heave he pulled himself into the saddle and raked the dun with spurs.

The animal lunged to a hard run. The snow ahead was bathed in a strong light, and he was reining toward the darkness of the ridge, wanting to be out of that light, when suddenly the dun stumbled.

The rifle's brittle *crack!* came the instant he instinctively tightened rein. He felt the gelding run strongly on. Then he was leaving the light behind and his animal was slogging up the face of the ridge through the trees.

Looking back, he saw a team pulling a wagon running in on the cabin. A pinpoint wink of powder flame stabbed at him from the wagon. He heard the bullet ricochet from the trunk of a pine close to his left.

He used his spurs again, used them mercilessly. And a craven fear was in him as he reached the top of the ridge and ran away.

Chapter 2

The hard jolting of the wagon spoiled that second shot, as it had the first, and as the rider faded from sight into the blackness along the face of the ridge Jim Harbour laid the rifle aside and came erect. The lean-to's far wall was a sheet of flame brightly lighting the trampled snow and the near end of the barn. He ran the team into that strong light, hauled sharply back on the reins and vaulted to the snow before the wheels had stopped rolling.

A wave of heat came at him as he ran in on the shelter. Flames were licking up along the stacked wood now, and in his panic he stood watching helplessly a moment. Then, suddenly furious, he threw his big frame against the lean-to's near wall, the impact of his shoulder splitting one of the boards.

He tore the board free and wheeled toward the stack of blazing corncobs. Using the board as a shovel, he dug into the mound, scooping part of it out into the snow. He thrust at it time after time until finally the last blazing cob was gone.

Dropping the board, he suddenly noticed

the far wall blazing fiercely almost to the line of the roof. Shielding his face with one arm, he kicked at the base of the outermost board. At the third hard pound of his boot the nails came loose. He was off-balance and staggered hard against the wall, the impact of his shoulder bringing a shower of sparks down on him. He beat at the shoulders of his coat and kicked at the second board, trying to loosen it. But, as Raoul Gardies had said last night, he had built well. The nails held.

He remembered the axe in the wagon then and, wheeling away from the heat and the glare, ran out across the snow. The blacks were nervous and started pulling away as he came in on them. He managed to get a hold on the brake-arm, throw it forward and then reach inside the empty bed and find the axe.

Back under the lean-to once again, he quickly chopped every board of the blazing wall from its ground studding. Tossing the axe aside then, he tore the first board from its roof stringer. His hand closed on the next's red-glowing edge and he grunted in pain. He put on his gloves, wiped them in the snow and then savagely tore loose the rest of the wall, hurling the flaming boards out into the snow.

Finally, badly winded, he began scooping snow onto the blazing ends of the stacked cordwood. He worked until exhaustion brought him to his knees. But with each thrust of his cupped hands the light of the blaze was weakening and he kept doggedly at it. In the end, when he was in complete darkness, he eased his weight forward against aching arms, hung his head and knew he had saved the cabin.

Presently, when his breathing had shallowed, he came wearily erect. He stood for several moments listening to the sibilant hissing of snow melting with the heat of the still smouldering and charred boards. Then, with halting steps, he trudged on around to the door, lifted its latch and tried to push it open.

It felt solid as a wall. He had put his shoulder against it, was about to force it, when suddenly he remembered the broken peg of its latch-bar. A wry smile came to his face then at recalling how he had yesterday morning been in too much of a hurry to make a new peg and fix the latch before leaving on the hunt. Thinking of the wind when he left the cabin, he had simply propped a chair against the inside of the door, tilting it so that its back would fall under the latch-block when the door closed. Here was probably the reason why the man he had briefly glimpsed had tried to fire his cabin from the outside rather than from the inside.

He patiently worked the door open now by lightly pushing and pulling on the handle. Finally he could reach around and lift the chair away. He went on in, carefully feeling along a table until his hand touched the base of a lamp. He had taken off the chimney and had a match in hand, about to light it, when he hesitated.

He was almost sure, almost but not quite, that he had recognized the man whose panicked flight had followed the line of the ridge. But he was positive he knew the animal that had carried the intruder away, for he had clearly seen its marking of an irregular dark hip blaze. He knew a dun gelding with that marking, one that wore a Crow Track shoulder brand. He had never seen anyone but Shep Nye ride the animal.

Now, thinking of what he knew of Shep Nye, he decided he would be safe in having a light. Once the lamp was going he laid a fire in the cook stove, then went out and drove his team to the barn.

There was something he had to think out, and he deliberated it as he was unhitching and feeding the mare and gelding. It was a forty minute ride to Crow Track. He would probably find Nye there at Rue's crew cabin. There were a number of things he could do if he went across there tonight, one of which was to repay Evan Rue in kind by trying to fire Crow Track's barn, its wagon shed or even the house itself. Yet, now that the anger in him had cooled, a time trained instinct for dealing with trouble warned him to choose his own time and place for a reckoning.

Jim Harbour's twenty-eight years had brought him a better than average acquaintance with violence, none of which he had relished, none of which had held strictly to the pattern of tonight's. Yet all was related to what had just now happened in some degree. And all of it had taught him the value of patience, so that now this hard-learned habit had its way with him, making him dismiss any thought of riding to Crow Track and instead sending him back to the cabin to cook his supper.

Toward midnight stars were shining through ragged gaps in the thinning clouds over the Arrowheads. By seven o'clock the next morning, as Jim Harbour saddled the gelding, a blaze of strong sunlight was touching the hill crests to the south with a glare hard to stare against.

At about the time Jim was heading toward the lower reach of his meadow, Evan Rue, Harry Talbot and Shep Nye were riding the foot of the pass road coming in on the Murchison homestead. It was then that Rue, who had been in one of his moody silences, said suddenly, "You two let me do the talking. No matter what happens. Understand, Shep?"

Nye was startled at being singled out so directly. "Sure I understand. But why the devil rawhide me any more than Harry here?"

Evan Rue was a gaunt slat of a man with a narrow face dominated by a wide and drooping mouse-colored moustache. His pale grey eyes now came around to fix Nye with a chill stare. "Because you've got no brains," he said bluntly, acidly. "If you had any you'd be forking another piece of horseflesh."

Shep Nye lifted his square-fingered hands outward in a gesture of helplessness. And Rue, seeing the man about to argue, snapped, "Harbour may know he nicked that brute last night. Let someone in town notice the gash on his rump, let the word get to Harbour and he could put two and two together."

"Why can't I say it was snagged on some brush? Or a —"

"Forget it," Rue interjected, reaching up to the soiled brim of his wide hat and pulling it lower across his eyes. "Now you let me handle Murchison and keep your lip buttoned."

Nye scowled at Talbot, shrugging in wonder at Rue's ill-humor. And when they shortly left the road and angled across toward the Murchison cabin, Talbot held back, drawling, "Better let him go ahead."

Smoke was lifting lazily from the cabin's chimney, rising straight into the clear bright air. Rue rode across the untracked snow to the cabin's front door, putting his animal so close to it that to announce his presence he simply took a boot from stirrup and gave the panel a solid kick.

He held his horse there, so that when old Tom Murchison opened the door a few seconds later he stepped sharply back, startled at finding a horse and rider almost inside his front room.

"Want a talk with you, Murchison."

Before the oldster could answer, his wife called from somewhere at the back of the cabin, "What is it, Tom?"

"Nothing, Carrie. Nothing." Murchison's lined face wore a worried look.

"Step outside," Rue told him.

"Then move that damn' crow bait away." The homesteader, who had ridden for Bit for eighteen years and had been pensioned last year by Raoul Gardies, had little use for Evan Rue. He had found his courage now and wasn't taking anything from the man. Rue saw that and moved his animal away a dozen or so feet.

Murchison had barely closed the door when Rue asked, "Did you hear I'm moving onto the Springs range?"

"Who hasn't heard? What did you do, stack the deck on that boy?"

Rue cocked his bony frame around in the saddle, letting the full weight of his pale-eyed glance coolly inspect the man for several seconds. Then, choosing to ignore the remark, he drawled, "I intend using all this grass between my place and the Springs. Which means this stretch."

"Who says you —"

"You'll either put in fence or have my cattle in your turnip patch," Rue interrupted, his voice toneless, without feeling.

Murchison's lined face turned livid. "You do that and I'll —"

"Either that or I buy you out." Rue was wasting no time on ceremony, allowing nothing to interrupt the bald stating of this ultimatum. "I can use your shack as a line camp. It's worth three hundred to me, along with title. Not a dollar more."

"A shack, is it?" Murchison roared apoplectically. "Why, you lanky devil. You ever set foot on this place or even let one of your mangy steers drift in here and whichever it is I'll blow it in two with buckshot."

It was as though Rue hadn't heard, for he calmly reined his horse on around, put his back to the man and headed for the road. "Think it over," he called as he went away. "I'll be by in a day or so to hear what you decide."

Murchison was shouting, swearing at them as they went on out the road. And Shep Nye, falling in with Talbot alongside Rue, scowled darkly, saying, "Damned if I'd take that from the old coot. Hear what he called you, boss? Why don't we go back and beat his scalp loose?"

Rue, typically, made no reply. And the heavy-bodied and slow witted Nye favored Talbot with a puzzled and angry glance.

The three Crow Track riders racked their animals at the *Niagara*'s tie-rail an hour and a half later, Rue going into the saloon while his two crewmen waited at the edge of the walk, avoiding the steady drip of the wooden awning where the snow was already melting in the strong sunlight.

Presently Rue rejoined them, saying sourly, "No luck there." He led the way down the walk and over the cross street to join eight men who had during this past hour ridden in singly or in pairs from the north and now waited in front of a building beyond the courthouse. At a word from Rue they climbed an outside stairway of the nearby building to a second floor office, entering a door with a weathered panel bearing the faded legend, *F. S. Shoemaker, Notary, Deeds, Wills, Titles.*

Shoemaker, a portly white-haired individual, was over-cordial in the way he greeted them. He showed considerable deference to Rue, offering him the chair behind his scarred deal desk.

After the door had closed behind the last man, Rue took the chair, looked around the room and asked sharply, "Where's Bailey? And who's seen Harrison and Crabtree?"

It was a man standing at the back window overlooking a littered vacant lot who quietly answered, "Bailey's wife is sick. He said to count him in. Harrison and Crabtree couldn't scrape together the money."

Rue's frowning glance ran over the others. "Well, we've culled the weak ones." He was once more abruptly regarding the man who had just spoken. "Didn't expect to find you here, Hapgood. Are you with us or against us?"

Hapgood was young, tall, his clothes the worse for wear. Yet there was a certain dignity and quiet strength in the way he met Rue's hard stare, and in the way he answered, "Sue and I have been waiting our chance.

Maybe this is it. I'm here to listen."

Evan Rue appeared undecided as to whether or not the answer suited him, but his glance finally moved away from Hapgood and he asked, "Any the rest of you thinking of backing out? Now's the time if you are."

For several seconds no one spoke or moved. Then one man standing near the door said uncertainly, "It's almighty late in the year to be settling cattle on strange range. This snow's only a sample of what's on the way in another month. Suppose these critters don't have time to learn their cover and their water? What's —"

"Did anyone ever claim it was going to be easy?" Rue interjected. "If a blizzard hits, every man of us gets out and rides twenty-four hours the day. Suppose we do get a heavy winter kill? We're still ahead of the game at the price we're paying. What's more important, we'll have land."

He paused, letting his words carry their weight. Then he was asking, "Anyone else got any steam to blow off?"

One or two men voiced negatives, others shook their heads. Whereupon Rue glanced up at Shoemaker. "Let's have it, Frank."

The notary cleared his throat, took off his spectacles and began polishing them with a dirt-greyed handkerchief. "You all know most of it," he began. "This man Pierce run into bad luck from the time he brought his herd across the Texas line. He started too late to begin with. Then a couple of skittery old bulls took the habit of stampedin' the bunch for no reason at all two or three nights a week. Pierce and his crew spent the last half the summer gatherin', pushing on a few miles, then having hell cut loose time after time before they found out the trouble and made skillet meat of them two bulls. They got here too late to sell on the market. Their beef was gaunt. Now Pierce'll unload for a song."

One of the men leaning against the up-street wall said, "Get on with it. We know all this."

"Well, there's not much more to —"

"Let me tell it." Rue took a pen from the notary's desk and began twirling it in his fingers. "Pierce makes a tally of three hundred sixty-four, subject to our count. His animals are shy on tallow but they're used to hustling for themselves and they'll winter average well. His price was fourteen the head, delivered on my range. But when I talked with him two days ago over in Bend he finally came down to twelve. I'd say he's got a buy we can't pass up."

"But the rest of the money," one man protested. "We got only about half enough. Where do we get the rest?"

"Not from the bank," another inserted dryly, his words bringing a few unamused laughs.

"And not from Wickwire," Rue told them. "I've just come from seeing him. So we know how he stands."

Just now a rotund man with the empty right sleeve of his blue Union coat folded back and sewn to the shoulder stepped from the room's door corner and from behind a man who blocked his view of Rue. He coughed gently, instantly getting the attention of all.

"Ev, I came along mostly to listen. But maybe we'd better get something squared away in the beginning, then I'll stay quiet."

His one hand pulled the coat aside and he hooked thumb in his belt that seemed the only support for a keg-like paunch. Then his glance swung deliberately from one man to another as he soberly stated, "None of you are breaking the law in doing this. But the first man that does break it gets locked up in my jail. That's got to be understood right off."

"Now listen, Bill," a man alongside the speaker protested. "Suppose I file, then move in on my quarter section? And suppose Bit comes along of a night, wrecks my place and tries to move me out? Do I go for the gun or tuck in my tail and run?"

"Yeah, Sheriff. How about it if Gardies sicks Neal on us?"

Eyeing Rue furtively, catching Rue's slight tilt of the head, the one-armed law man answered, "I was elected to uphold the law. There's your answer, simple as that. If you're within the law, if you've filed and got certificate, I'll arrest anyone that tries to push you off."

"You gonna tell that to Gardies, Parks?" the man by the window, Hapgood, gently queried.

Before Bill Parks could reply, Evan Rue said tonelessly, "Let's cut the wranglin' and get on with this. Bill's given you straight answers. He's said he'll see our rights protected. Gardies knows the law and doesn't have to be told."

"Where was the law a year ago when Lew Neal warned me off Porcupine Ridge?"

"This is now, not last year," Rue stated. "We've got a new sheriff, we're through taking our rawhiding from Bit. So we go straight from here to the courthouse. We file. We take our pick of that open range north and east. We stick together. If they drive us to it, we burn some powder."

He gave Shoemaker a glance. "Every man here signs this contract with Pierce when he hands over his money. You'll get a receipt.

I've put down the amount you're each to pay, according to how many cattle you said you wanted four days ago."

"Hell, Evan, I can't hold up my end. Where's the money to come from?" someone asked. "All I could scrape together was two hundred forty dollars."

"I'd hoped Wickwire would loan us what we need." Rue shrugged. But then his thin face shed its severe cast for the first time since he had come into the room. He had been waiting for this question, and now he played what he hoped was his trump card by telling them, "Guess I forgot to mention it. But Pierce has agreed to take half his money now, the other half one year from the day we sign. At no interest. It's a good deal for him, it's better than good for us. Now does that stiffen your weak knees even if we couldn't swing the whole thing at once?"

Despite his sarcasm and the well-hidden resentment some of these men felt toward him, there was a murmur of surprised approval. One man even crossed to the desk and reached out saying, "Hand over that pen. I'm signing."

It was Hapgood, who had stayed at the window and not come forward as the others were now doing, who abruptly queried, "How good is that contract, Rue? Shoemaker's no lawyer."

"He's a notary." Rue was having a hard time controlling his temper, for Hapgood was respected here and his opinion might sway the others, two of whom were already hesitating.

Rue saw that he must say something to clinch this and, getting out of the chair, told them, "From now on out we can hold up our heads. Bit's had its day and the man that hangs back from a deal like this has his head twisted on backwards."

He handed the pen to the man across the desk, uncorked a bottle of ink and reached over to take the contract from Shoemaker and offer it to the signer. "Leave the top line open for me, Red. Next year when we see all that range up north filled with our brands, I want to be able to say I was the first to begin whittlin' Gardies down."

They were convinced finally and crowded in on the desk. All but Hapgood, who quietly crossed to the door and left the room.

Renee Gardies brought the mare to a stand at the street's edge in front of Mrs. Schwab's rooming house and was winding the reins about the buggy's empty whip-socket when she heard the house door slam. Glancing up, she saw her brother coming down the porch steps.

Phil Gardies' thin and handsome face wore an expression of outright delight as he hurried down the path and waded the snow to stand below her. "Lord, you're a grown woman," he breathed in an awed way. "A damn' beautiful woman."

She laughed, her eyes bright with happiness. "Still the same charmer," she said. "Now I know I'm really home."

Phil reached up and lifted her from the buggy. He kissed her and she hugged him tightly a moment, her doubts beginning to leave her then as she pushed away and studied his face.

He looks older, older than he should. The thought was disquieting and she immediately told herself, *But he's still the same.* An understanding of how difficult these years of her absence must have been for him put a gentleness in her tone now as she said, "You're thin as a rail, Phil."

"Still growing." He pulled one of the reins free and stepped over to tie to the hitching-post. Then, coming back to put an arm about her waist, he turned her toward the house. "Come in. We'll get some coffee, take over the parlor and talk ourselves out."

"Can't we just walk?" She looked down at the bulky overshoes she was wearing and laughed. "Unless I look too much like a scrub woman."

"I've been waiting to show this town a scrub woman like you. Sure let's walk."

They started up the path leading to the center of town, arm in arm, Phil shortly saying, "Let's have a sample of your new lingo, kid. Tell me what day it is."

"I could tell you and you still wouldn't know." She held his arm tighter. "But I do know that day after tomorrow's Thanksgiving. And I know you're spending it with us out home."

"Whoa now." He slowed his pace, his expression sobering as he glanced down at her. "Don't tell me you've turned missionary."

"No, Phil. But I've talked with dad about this. He's . . . well, he's coming around."

"You could always make him do anything." He shook his head. "Nope. It would last for a day or two, then one of us would start it all off again. I went out there when he was hurt, tried to help Madge look after him. As soon as he got his strength back we tangled like we always do. I won't go through it again."

She walked along in silence for several moments, finally saying, "He's in trouble, Phil. Or thinks he is. And he's sick. His heart's been giving him trouble."

"So Doc Emery was telling me. I'm sorry as can be." He meant it. "But you say trouble. Something besides his heart and legs?"

"He imagines Rue is going to try something."

He breathed a long sigh, drawling, "I ought to be horse whipped for that, kid. But damn Rue. He was so all-fired sure of himself."

"It's done now, so let's don't talk about it." Wanting to change the subject, Renee asked, "Do you have a decent room, Phil? Do you get enough to eat?"

"Yes on both counts." As an afterthought, he said, "No telling why I stick around, though. I ought to go some place else, get work and forget Alder."

"I could loan you money if you need it," she said gently. "A lot of it if you need it."

"Thanks." He smiled crookedly. "Dad's listed all my sins for you? How much I drink, how I'm making out with the fair sex? Think I'd be a good risk?"

She tried to ignore his bitterness. "Dad forgets he was young once. He forgets until some trouble like this comes along. Then he —"

"Trouble?" he cut in. "You said that before. What trouble?"

"He thinks Rue may move out from Crow Track toward the Springs."

"That's the talk going the rounds. Not only

about Rue but about others off to the north of Owl Creek and Porcupine."

Renee looked up at her brother in a wondering way. "You don't care, Phil?"

He shrugged. "Care? Maybe I do in a way. But I'm one of the down-and-outers now, Renee. I know how they feel everytime they ride those fifteen miles from here to Owl and realize it all belongs to one man while they grub around up in those breaks watching their crops dry up and blow away and their steers eating weeds."

"But who asked them to settle up there?" she countered hotly. "Aren't they trash, all of them?"

"No, not all. There are a few like Pete Hapgood and Bailey who came in without knowing what they were up against. Pete sold a farm back in Illinois and came here thinking he could pick up a good piece of land. He can't. Now he's stranded."

"There's unfairness in everything." She wasn't giving in to his argument. "Would you want dad to let these settlers come in and take everything away from him? If he did let a few come, wouldn't there be others? Until in the end he'd have nothing left?"

He was abruptly smiling again, squeezing her arm. "Here we've been together three or four minutes and we're arguing something we can't change one way or the other. Let's talk about you, about —"

"But this is a serious thing. Serious for all of us. Dad's so convinced something's going to happen that he's trying to hire that man Harbour to work for him."

Phil Gardies' look was one of stunned wonderment. Then he was suddenly laughing. "Now there's just a sample. One day Harbour's dust under the old man's feet. The next he gets offered a job." He shook his head in bafflement.

"Do you know Harbour?"

"Barely. Why?"

"Dad seems to think he could keep Rue in line. How right is he?"

"Halfway right. Harbour's made Rue eat crow once at least."

Phil had answered almost disinterestedly, for his glance had gone up the street a moment ago. And now he told her, "Here comes someone who may have a few answers. Pete Hapgood, the man I was mentioning, the one from Illinois."

"What could he tell us?"

"Rue called some sort of meeting this morning in Shoemaker's office. Pete might've been there. Let's see what he has to say."

As Shoemaker's office was emptying, Rue

caught Bill Parks' eye. The sheriff came over to the desk and Rue told him, "Stick around." Shortly, as the last man went down the stairs and Shoemaker closed the door, Rue asked, "Mind leaving us alone for a few minutes, Frank?"

"No, not at all. Make yourselves comfortable."

Shoemaker took his hat down from a deer-antler rack along the wall and was opening the door when Rue spoke again. "Nye and Talbot are down there somewhere. You might tell them I'll be along in a few minutes."

"Sure will."

The law man and Rue listened to the solid clump of the notary's boots against the steps outside. And as they faded Rue said affably, "You laid it right on the line, Bill. Made it look real respectable and law abiding. Much obliged for the help."

Parks ignored the thanks, reacting differently than Rue had supposed he would. "I don't like any part of it, Ev. Half these men are hardcases or tramps. They don't want to homestead any more than I want to learn blacksmithin'. The rest are plain farmers and don't belong in cow country."

"But it all adds up to what we want." Rue was plainly startled, nevertheless went on to explain patiently, "It takes at least six homesteads to swing this the way I want to see it go, to cover all the likely spots between Owl and Porcupine. If you can't find eight good men you damn' well take those you can get. Which is what I did."

"You've sure got some weak ones." The one-armed man shook his head dubiously. "Take Ames and Dooley. They're the kind I might get a dodger on any day. If they've got the money to put up for this they robbed a bank to —"

"They don't have it, Bill."

At Parks' puzzled look, Rue went on, "This is between you and me, but when I first got wind of Pierce and his cattle I went to the bank and took out a mortgage. For improvements, I told Baker. As it worked out, the money just about covered my share in the deal plus enough extra to put up some for Ames and Dooley. Like you say, they're not what they let on to be. They've hired on with me at straight wages, just those two. They may stick around for only a year or less, then let their claims drop. Meantime, they're the kind that'll make Bit think twice before trying to run our bunch off. If Bit wants trouble, those two'll earn their wages twice over. When they pull out, if they do, I may take their land over."

The sheriff's eyes were suddenly bright

with anger. Seeing that, Rue asked gruffly, "What ails you?"

"It's just come over me that some of us are being played for suckers, me included." Parks' soft drawl was deceptive. "Up until now I've bought into this because I wanted to see Gardies whittled down."

"That's what you are seeing, isn't it?"

"Is it? Or are the pack of us building Crow Track into a big outfit for you?"

The shelving line of Rue's jaw thrust forward. "Just what the devil are you trying to say, Bill?"

"It was agreed you'd take over that strip of grass to the east, six times as much as any other man's getting." The sheriff's tone was cool, sharp. "Now you say you hope Dooley and Ames may hand you even more. The rest wind up with two-bit layouts. As for me, I wind up with not one damned thing."

"You've got your badge, haven't you? The more this country's opened up the better chance you have of keeping your star."

"It's a job, nothing else. Look, man, I can take —"

"Look yourself, Bill," Rue cut in. "Aren't you forgetting something?"

Parks' expression underwent a subtle change. He seemed to become a man of less stature, to be shrinking into himself, as Rue continued softly, "So you were one of Jim Andrews' raiders, were you? Ask any man on the street who heard your campaign speeches and he'll tell how you helped Andrews steal that train in Marietta and fire those bridges below Chattanooga. How you had your arm whacked by a Rebel bayonet there in the woods when Andrews was captured. How you nearly bled to death while you were getting back to the Union lines."

He laughed softly. "Bill, you're with us and you'll stay with us. You'll back us against Gardies. Unless . . ." He paused a moment, adding weight to the word . . . "Unless you want the story to get around about how you really lost that arm. I was there, Bill. Remember?"

Parks' face showed a sickly pallor now as he muttered feebly, "Lay off, will you?"

"Remember how long you were out of your head there in the hospital? I've never told you some of the things you said those nights when you hollered like a stuck pig. Maybe I ought to tell you now, Bill."

"All right, all right," the law man put in miserably, helplessly. "I'll go along with you. You can count on me all the way."

Rue, in the friendliest possible way, came around the desk, put an arm about Parks' shoulders and turned him toward the door.

"Everything's working out just fine," he drawled. "Now don't you worry about a blessed thing, Bill."

Jim Harbour was a mile from Alder when the ten deliberate mid-morning notes of the courthouse bell drifted to him across the still, bright air. The black carried him on at a steady jog, the animal's hoof strikes deadened by the heavy snow except for an occasional splashing where the track dipped across low ground. It was thawing. If it stayed this warm the snow would be gone in two or three more days.

These past two hours had been a sobering interval for Harbour, for he had been thinking back upon last night's firing of his cabin, and upon his talk with Raoul Gardies two nights ago. The reality of the past forty hours lay in sharp contrast to his mood of day before yesterday when leaving his meadow at the height of the storm to begin his hunt.

Then he'd had a feeling of release, of real pleasure on looking forward to what the day might bring. After these past months of unbroken before-dawn to after-dark laboring, the storm had brought an enforced idleness, or at least a postponement of the endless hard work. That work had put a cabin, a barn, a corral and four huge stacks of timothy hay across the big meadow that had last spring been unmarked by anything except a few clumps of scrub-oak and, down by the creek, the small soddy that had sheltered him last winter.

He had felt two mornings ago that he had passed a turning point in his life. For now he had a home, he was no longer at a loose end. He had accomplished a great deal more than adding to his reputation as a town marshal, or possibly adding to his reputation as a killer. He had more than the savings from his wages to show for three years of his life.

Yet in a minute, even in seconds last night, his feeling of security had been shattered. It still awed him to think of what could have happened had he driven up to the meadow a quarter of an hour later than he had. The cabin would have been gone, perhaps the barn along with it. Yet his having saved the cabin didn't alter the fact that things were not as they had seemed day before yesterday.

These two hours of soberly facing the facts had driven him to a decision. What he had decided presently took him straight along Alder's main street as far as the *Niagara*'s wide awning. He saw three Crow Track ponies standing there at the rail. One was a dun with a grey hip blaze.

As he turned from the center of the muddy

street his glance ran along the walks. Coming in to the rail beyond the Crow Track animals, he plainly saw the raw gash his bullet had last night channeled along the dun's rump. He deliberated something then that made him reach up and unbuckle his heavy coat so that it hung loose. And now as he stepped down into the slush a wariness tightened his nerves and made him not look at his hands as he tied reins to the rail.

He stepped onto the walk, glancing both ways along it, not seeing what he was looking for. No onlooker could have detected the care with which he approached the saloon's glassed door. Nevertheless he moved quickly past the *Niagara*'s near window and he stood to one side of the door before he opened it and went in.

The saloon was empty except for the apron, the Negro cook working over the stove behind the lunch bar and two customers he had never seen before. He asked the apron, "George in?" and got the answer, "Ought to be in his office."

Harbour found Wickwire sitting in shirtsleeves behind the desk in the back room. "Look who's here," the saloonman said cordially, nodding to a chair at the far end of the desk. He caught the sober set of his visitor's face then. "Whose funeral you headed for?"

Jim smiled thinly. "Not my own, I hope." He tilted his head toward the front of the building. "Shep Nye's gelding is out there. Know where I can find him?"

Wickwire's expression at once turned serious. He shook his head. "No. But Rue was in here something over an hour ago. Wanting to borrow money, believe it or not."

"Did he get it?"

"He didn't. He wanted a cool two thousand, by the way."

Whistling softly, Jim asked, "What's wrong with the bank?"

"He didn't say. Didn't even say why he wanted so much. We didn't get around to discussing it."

Jim shrugged, seeming to dismiss the thought of Rue. "Then you don't know where I'd find Nye?"

"Not so fast, man," Wickwire told him. "There's more to it than Rue having been in. On my way from the hotel I saw our soldier sheriff standing down by Shoemaker's office. With Hapgood, Ames, that slippery joker Dooley and several more north country men."

"Should that mean something?"

The saloonman lifted his hands from the desk, let them fall again. "It could and it couldn't. I was simply remarking on the fact that Bill Parks was in on a gatherin' of Rue's clan. Which is making it pretty public."

"What're you trying to say, George?"

"That Rue and Parks are old friends. That they wore the blue together at Shiloh and other places. That they'll be like brothers if Rue forces a showdown with Gardies."

"And it looks like he might be doing just that," Harbour said quietly.

George Wickwire was quick to sense something behind his words, for he said, "Something's happened," not putting it in the form of a question.

"Something has. Someone tried to burn me out last night. Someone I got a look at."

The gambler's eyes had come wider open in astonishment. "Who?"

"Nye."

Wickwire's fists clenched, came open again. When he said nothing, Jim spoke once more. "So you're lucky I didn't take you up on your offer yesterday."

"The offer still stands. In fact, you're empty-headed if you don't take me up on it."

Jim was turning toward the door as he said, "I may be back later and talk about it."

"Where you going?"

"Out to take a look around."

"Wait. I'll go with you. Need some air."

Wickwire rose and reached to a coat rack standing behind the desk, lifting down a shoulder holster and strapping it to his chest before putting on his coat and joining Jim at the door.

Jim knew what his friend intended and said in irritation, "I don't need a wet nurse. You keep out of this."

"Of course." The gambler led the way on into the saloon.

"I mean it, George. Don't buy in." Jim came even with the saloonman as they were halfway along the bar. He reached the door ahead of Wickwire.

Pulling open the door, he was about to step out onto the walk when, looking toward the street, he saw Rue, Nye and Talbot coming obliquely toward the saloon from the opposite walk.

He halted so sharply that Wickwire jolted into him. And now as he stepped aside to shrug out of his heavy coat and lay it over the back of a chair at a nearby table, he told the gambler, "If I'm able to walk back in here to get this, or even crawl, I'll take your offer."

"Now you're talking."

"Only let me do this my way. Alone."

"Sure, sure," came Wickwire's amused rejoinder.

Jim knew it was pointless to argue the matter further. Wickwire had decided that the odds would probably be against his friend and, typically, was setting out to correct those odds. He would undoubtedly make enemies if he took sides in this, yet that didn't seem to matter.

Pulling open the door, feeling the weight of the holstered .44 Colt's at his thigh, Jim moved out onto the walk. He was aware of Wickwire walking away along the front of the saloon as he sauntered to the walk's edge watching the approach of the Crow Track men.

They didn't at once notice him. They were still thirty yards from their horses now as Nye said something that made both Talbot and Rue laugh. Then all at once Evan Rue glanced his way. His stride stiffened without breaking. He evidently spoke to the other two, for Nye's startled glance immediately whipped across to Jim.

They came straight on, separating and walking toward their animals as they neared the rails. All three pointedly ignored Jim, who stood beyond Nye's dun. He let the Crow Track man pull the reins loose, let him even lift a boot to stirrup before he asked clearly, not loudly, "Been lighting any more fires, Shep?"

Nye's thick body went motionless. He lowered his boot and looked around in mock surprise. "How's that?"

Rue and Talbot had heard Jim speak and were looking his way now, all but their heads and shoulders blocked from Jim's view by Nye's gelding. Jim saw at once that he had put himself at a disadvantage, saw also that this could have been avoided. He was wondering how he could deal with the other two Crow Track men when he suddenly noticed that George Wickwire stood down there near the edge of the walk so as to have a clear view of both Talbot and Rue. And a feeling of strong relief and gratefulness rose in him as he spoke to Nye again, saying softly, "Come here, Shep."

Nye's heavy frame straightened. "Why the hell should I?"

This interchange was falling into an old and familiar pattern, one Jim Harbour had thought he would never again be following. He was dealing in violence once more, not wanting it but nevertheless knowing it could be no other way.

Suddenly deciding to end the preliminaries he drawled, "You won't be needing your coat for this, Shep. Shed it."

Indecision and surprise were etched indelibly on Nye's thick-featured face. His wary glance shifted momentarily to Jim's thigh.

Catching that, wanting to hurry this, Jim reached to the buckle of his shell-belt. "We'll shed these, too," he said. "Or do we use them?"

A look of cunning, of satisfaction came to Nye's narrow-set eyes now. He unbuttoned his coat, took it off and laid it across his saddle. "Mind telling me what this is all about?" he asked tonelessly.

"Tell you later, Shep."

Jim stepped down off the walk now, ducked under the rail and came to a stand within two paces of Nye. He unbuckled the shell-belt but held it about his waist as he waited for Nye to move. The man wore a Colt's high at his belt, handle-foremost and wedged against hip bone. And now, very carefully, he reached up to lift his weapon clear. He tossed it to the walk so that it skidded across the planks and banged against the *Niagara*'s wall.

Reaching over and hanging belt and gun on the tie-rail, Jim sensed Nye suddenly diving at him. He had been expecting this, or something like it. He had even halfway turned his back to invite such a move. Seeing the other's move now, he instantly began wheeling away.

But the boot that took his weight slipped across the mud and he fell awkwardly to his knees. Nye hurtled into him, sending him sprawling. As he tried to roll out of the way the Crow Track man kicked at him, the boot catching him hard and solidly in the chest.

He was gagging for a breath and dropping his left shoulder against the pain of his ribs as he crouched, wheeled clear finally and stood up. Nye's kick had proclaimed what kind of a fight this was to be, and now as they stood warily, each waiting for the other's move, Jim heard George Wickwire's voice saying tonelessly, "Gentlemen, let's not interfere."

Shep Nye was almost a head shorter than Jim, but heavier. He could also move faster than Jim had suspected and, having seen evidence of this, Jim came at the man now in a half-crouch, feinted with his left and stepped quickly back. Nye dropped a shoulder, expecting a following blow, and that instant Jim once again jabbed with his left. His fist glanced off the man's shoulder, yet the force of it was enough to throw Nye momentarily off-balance. And in the split-second he was trying to get his footing Jim's right snapped full and hard against his mouth.

Nye's head came down between his heavy shoulders and he charged, arms outstretched. Jim wheeled out of his way. Yet Nye, as though having expected this, suddenly swung his left arm in a vicious back-handed blow that caught Jim hard on the side of the face. Then, before Jim could move, Nye swung sharply at him and lifted a knee at his groin.

The slippery footing saved Jim now as it had several moments ago worked against him. For Nye's boot slipped as he wheeled, and his knee glanced off the inside of Jim's thigh with a numbing jolt.

The Crow Track man was close in now, there was no room to hit him squarely. So Jim brought an elbow around in a tight arc that rocked Nye's head sharply and made him back off. And before Nye could get his balance Jim connected with a hard right to the face and a glancing blow with his left.

Nye was hurt. He stumbled backward into the tie-rail, outspread arms keeping him from falling. Seeing Jim coming at him, he ducked under the pole. The walk's edge collided with his shins and he fell back across the planks. He rolled quickly away, Jim following, vaguely noticing that men were crowding the walk in front of the adjoining building.

Nye saw that he was cornered and came to his knees, then dove at Jim's legs. Jim sidestepped, and it was then that Nye tried to get to his feet. He had almost straightened, arms crossed before his face, when a hard uppercut lifted him fully erect. An instant later

Jim's right smashed at his jaw. Nye staggered into him, he shoved the man's limp bulk away and then put the weight of another full swing behind Nye's bent-kneed stagger.

The Crow Track man fell suddenly backward and into the *Niagara*'s window. It collapsed in a loud jangling of glass. The sill caught him and he toppled back off the walk and into the saloon. Jim kicked away the ragged edges of glass along the sill and reached in to take a hold on one of the man's boots. He dragged Nye back across the window's sill and onto the walk once more.

Nye, groggy and badly hurt, nevertheless kicked out at him with his free leg, his spur ripping the left sleeve of Jim's shirt and gashing his arm from elbow to wrist, making him lose his grip.

As Jim's right hand closed instinctively about his bleeding arm, Shep Nye somehow managed to roll over and start rising. Jim stepped in on him, kneed him in the chest. And with the man's body jolted upright he threw all the weight of his powerful shoulders behind first a left, then a full smashing right at Nye's jaw.

Nye's heavy frame went loose. His arms fell to his sides. Jim could have hit him again but didn't as he staggered blindly, stumbling out across the walk.

He lost his footing as he reached the edge of the planks. He fell limply out and into the tie-rail. It cracked, split and came crashing down with his limp weight into the mud and the slush.

Chapter 3

Shep Nye's fall into the street had broken the tie-rail. Its far end collapsed into the mud now, splashing Talbot's mare so that the animal reared back, throwing Talbot into Nye's dun. Harry Talbot swore, tried to push from between the two animals and was kicked in the thigh by the dun.

He finally broke free, limped quickly around to where Nye lay face down in the slush and rolled him onto his back. "He's alive," he said. "Don't ask me why."

Jim Harbour stood breathing hard, feeling the blood dripping from the fingers of his left hand. He was looking at Rue now, aware of George Wickwire standing nearby along the walk and of a dozen or so others beyond. Rue was as Jim had last seen him, alongside his horse. And as their glances locked the Crow Track owner's pale eyes blazed with a killing hate and humiliation.

There was no need for anything to be said, for the voicing of threat or warning, Jim was thinking. Shep Nye's battered hulk lying there in the sun at the street's edge was more eloquent than any words could have been.

Evan Rue seemed to understand this, for his glance abruptly swung away and to Talbot. "Take him to Doc Emery's," he said tonelessly. "Stay with him."

He ignored his crewman then, and ignored Jim as he eyed Wickwire. "Have a look at our tinhorn, all of you," he said in a tone roughened by impotent rage.

For the first time Jim noticed that Wickwire held a gun in his hand. It was hanging loosely at his side, pointed at the walk. And now the gambler looked down at it, seeming surprised. Deliberately, he pulled open his coat and holstered the weapon, then glanced around at the group crowding the walk. His enigmatic stare singled out two men he had earlier seen waiting below Shoemaker's office down the street.

"I take it there's a difference of opinion here," he drawled. "Some of you may object to my having kept friend Rue from jumping Harbour. If so, I'm prepared to argue the matter."

Someone at the back fringe of the crowd said quietly, "I'll argue it, too."

It was Phil Gardies who had spoken. And Jim, singling him out, saw Renee Gardies standing beside him. Her glance met Jim's, showing a mute hurt and bewilderment.

He was trying to understand the emotion so strongly written on her striking face, trying to understand it in the light of their parting yesterday, when Wickwire spoke again:

"You're included in that invitation, Rue."

The gambler's cool glance was full on the Crow Track man, and for a moment it appeared from Rue's rigid stance that he was about to carry this further. Yet he appeared uncertain, never before having seen this side of Wickwire's nature.

Finally the doubt in him made him turn and climb to the saddle. He looked across to Talbot to say gruffly, "Don't just stand there." Then he wheeled his animal out from the rail with a hard jerk on the reins, rode into the street and away.

Wickwire came along the walk now to kick Nye's Colt's out so that it splashed into the slush close to Talbot. He reached over and lifted Jim's belt and holstered .44 from the broken rail, his look worried as he took in Jim's bleeding arm.

"Let's get that fixed in a hurry."

The two of them turned toward the *Niagara*'s door, Jim telling his friend, "I owe you for some glass."

The gambler's face lost its seriousness for the first time.

"Watching that was worth ten busted windows," he said, smiling broadly. "You don't owe me a thing. It's on the house."

None of the onlookers had so much as moved until now, as the saloon's door swung shut behind Jim and Wickwire. A few men moved in to stand looking down at Nye. Others began talking, and as a man near Renee said in an awed way, "The roof sure fell in on Shep," she pulled at her brother's sleeve to ask in a hushed way, "Will he live, Phil?"

"Probably, more's the pity."

"Why were they fighting?"

"Can't tell." Phil looked over the heads of the men blocking his view of the saloon doorway. "I'd like to know, like to see Harbour." He looked down at Renee, asking, "Were you going on back home?"

"I . . . I'd thought we could spend the day together," she said hesitantly.

"We will. But we'll spend it out home. You go on back, get the buggy and get started. I'll catch up with you."

Her eyes were all at once bright with happiness. "You mean it, Phil? You're coming back home?"

"If the old man'll have me. Or maybe even if he won't. It might be better not to let him know I'm to be around."

"We'll talk about it," she said, squeezing

his arm, then turning away as she added, "Hurry."

He watched her a moment as she walked on down toward the intersection. Glancing up the walk again, he saw that men were hurrying toward the crowd from both directions along the walk and from across the street. One of these late arrivals was Sheriff Parks, who came running from the hotel corner calling, "What's wrong here?"

He roughly shouldered several men aside, tried to push Phil Gardies out of his way. But Phil stood as he was, and the law man gave him an angry scowl as he stepped around him and hurried on, coming abreast the broken tie-rail just as three men were lifting Nye's limp bulk from the mud.

"Who saw this happen?" . . . Parks' tone was officious, quarrelsome . . . "Come on, speak up. Who did this to Nye?"

Phil Gardies made his way through the crowd as the sheriff was listening to a garbled account of the fight. Joining the traffic entering the saloon, he heard Parks ask loudly, testily, "Where'd Harbour go? Where'll I find him?"

The *Niagara*'s bar was crowded. Phil sauntered over to lean against the end of the long pine counter, listening to the hum of talk filling the room, looking for Harbour and

Wickwire and not seeing them.

"Drinks on the house, Phil. What'll it be, rye?"

Phil looked around. "Nothing now, thanks."

The barkeep had been reaching for a bottle, knowing his man. Phil's reply made his face go slack with wonder, as though he doubted his hearing. "You'll fall apart, man," he said then as he went along the counter to wait on another customer.

Phil Gardies' face, older looking than his twenty-one years and already showing lines of dissipation, colored slightly as he caught the meaning behind the words. But then he forgot them as he looked back with relish upon what he had seen on the street these past five minutes. He was prepared to enjoy the next five as well, for he was certain this affair was far from finished.

What he had been expecting to happen did happen a quarter-minute later as the *Niagara*'s street door slammed so loudly that every man in the big room turned at the sound.

Bill Parks stood just inside the door. He waited out a deliberate moment until he had the room's full attention. Then: "Where's Harbour? Damned if he half kills a man and gets away with it."

Someone answered, "He's back gettin' his

arm fixed, back with George."

Parks had taken two strides toward the rear of the room when the door to Wickwire's office abruptly opened and the gambler and Harbour appeared. They were talking quietly as they came along the bar, Harbour sticking some folded papers in shirt-pocket and then rolling down the bloody sleeve of his shirt over his bandaged arm. He carried his coat over his good arm.

Neither man at first noticed the room's stillness or the sheriff standing there at the center of the floor. Then finally Wickwire looked up and saw Parks. Nudging Harbour, he said, "Morning, Sheriff. Something I can do for you?"

Parks ignored the question, bluntly stating, "Harbour, you're under arrest."

Jim Harbour's lean face showed a strong surprise. "Now am I?" He had stopped several strides short of the law man. "Do I get to know what for?"

"I'm locking you up till I know how bad Nye's hurt. Until I know if he wants to swear out a warrant."

A slow smile patterned Jim's face, though his blue eyes held a chill look. "Anyone tell you what it was all about, Sheriff?"

"No one seems to know."

"Then until you do know you don't have

a reason for locking me up."

"Like hell I don't." Parks' narrow jaw tightened in anger. "You're talking to the law. I say you don't have the right to beat a man almost to death and get away with it. Why'd you do it?"

"Ask Nye."

"He can't talk. Maybe he never will talk again."

Jim only shrugged. And Wickwire, closely watching this, saw that the one-armed man was being prodded to the verge of doing something foolish. "Both of you calm down," he quickly inserted. "Bill, last night Nye tried to fire Jim's cabin. Jim surprised him at it and he got away. But there was no mistake about it being Nye."

Parks' belligerence weakened before surprise, then uncertainty. He had sensed for several moments that he was unaccountably beyond his depth in this situation, that he was somehow acting too hastily and had put himself in the wrong. Now, thankful that his difficulty was resolving itself so simply, he bridled, "Why didn't somebody tell me this before?"

He stared uneasily at Harbour, knowing that half the men at the bar had lost a measure of respect for him, knowing that he must make the best of it. "What's Nye got against you?"

"Ask him. Or ask your friend Rue."

The sheriff's face took on color. "Rue wouldn't have no cause to try a damn' fool trick like burning a man out," he stated. Then, to cover his confusion, he asked, "You want to prefer any charges?"

"The charges have already been preferred, Sheriff."

Someone at the bar laughed softly. Others were smiling. Parks, once again furious, glared at the offenders. Then, since there was little he could do beyond attempting a graceful exit, he growled, "We'll see what Nye's got to say," and turned and stalked back out the door.

The room slowly filled with the sound of voices once more. And as the tension eased away, Phil Gardies digested the fact of Shep Nye's move against Harbour, adding it to what Pete Hapgood had told him before the fight. And he knew with no doubt whatsoever that this morning marked the beginning of real trouble for Bit.

He was watching Harbour now and shortly saw the man pull on his coat, speak briefly to Wickwire and then head for the door. He left the bar, following Harbour onto the walk and along it in the direction of the cross street below.

Once they were clear of the thinning crowd,

he called, "Where to, Harbour?"

Jim glanced around, slowing his pace. "Got something to do at the courthouse."

Coming even with the taller man, Gardies asked, "Mind if I tag along?"

"Not at all."

They walked on together, Phil shortly saying, "Hope you put him to sleep for keeps."

"I don't." Jim smiled meagerly. "He'll come around. He's tough."

"But not tough enough." Phil eyed Jim soberly, continuing, "Which is what someone else seems to think. Renee was in this morning and told me about the old man seeing you night before last."

He waited for some response. Getting none beyond a brief, enigmatic look, he said, "You're still holding out?"

"What do you think?"

Phil sighed gustily. "Don't blame you. But after what's happened you might do worse than take the job."

They came to the intersection and waded the melting snow and the puddles to the walk fronting the hotel. Phil sensed a near hostility in Jim and, understanding it, was once again the one to end an awkward silence. "It begins to add up, doesn't it? First me handing Rue the Springs layout, then Rue trying to burn you out. Now Rue calling his pack together this morning."

"George was wondering about that."

"You haven't heard what they're doing?" At Jim's shake of the head, Phil added, "I ran into Pete Hapgood. He'd just come from Shoemaker's office, which is where they met."

He went on then to repeat what Hapgood had told him just before the fight. The details were all there and he gave them briefly, finishing by saying, "So it looks like we're in for it. Bit, I mean. Inside a week Rue and his bunch will have moved these cattle between the Springs and Crow Track and on out across Porcupine as far as Owl Creek."

"Which the law says they can do," Jim stated dryly.

"I know. But that'll only be the beginning. Come summer and they'll begin crowding us further. Rue will take as much as he can. This is what he's been waiting fifteen years to do. He hates the old man."

"Some others I could mention don't particularly like him."

"So they don't. You for one. Well, I'd probably go along with you if he wasn't my father." Over a moment's pause as they passed a woman, tipping their hats to her, Phil added, "The funny part of it is I want to help him now that the chips are down.

Now, before Rue gets too strong, before it's too late."

They were approaching the courthouse, a brick building little different from the false-fronted stores flanking it to either side. And as Jim turned from the walk to take the steps to its wide doorway, Gardies said, "I'm going out there today and have Neal put me to work. But I wish it was to be you, not Neal, who'd be telling me what to do."

Jim paused in the act of pushing open the courthouse door and looked down at Phil. "You're like your sister, expecting you can make things over at the drop of a hat. People don't forget that easy, Gardies."

A rueful smile patterned Phil Gardies' face. "You can't forget. I can because I've got to. Well, if you change your mind you know what to do."

With a spare nod, Jim said, "Don't look for it to happen," and went on into the building.

Gardies continued on along the street, heading for the livery. He was so absorbed in thinking back over the past half hour that he several times unknowingly waded through puddles formed by the morning's quick thaw. Two days ago, or even yesterday, he had regarded Jim Harbour as just another of the many people he occasionally saw in Alder whose resentment he instinctively expected because he was Raoul Gardies' son. Yesterday he would have ridiculed the idea of the man ever siding with Bit in any trouble whatsoever. Yet Harbour had today lined himself on Bit's side whether he liked it or not, if by accident.

Phil was just now experiencing an old and unfamiliar sense of pride in having so impulsively backed Wickwire's ultimatum to the crowd just after the fight. These past months of disappointment, disheartenment and self abuse had so weakened and embittered him that even a small thing like the voicing of those few words in the hearing of the crowd had made him feel a better and a cleaner man. There had been no bravado in him. He knew he would have sided with the gambler had Rue or anyone else among the onlookers chosen to take exception to the man's blunt challenge.

For the first time in days, in months, Phil Gardies felt he had been completely honest with himself. He had unpredictably acted in an honorable way, not as a weakling. Seeing Renee, having her with him, had in part influenced him. Yet another thing had been his decision to forget his pride and return to Bit. And now as he waded the street's mud, crossing to the livery barn, he was suddenly anxious to put this town and all it meant behind him.

Twenty minutes later, astride a Bit horse that had been left at the livery several days ago, he took a trail that angled from the main road north across the bench. The trail would save him perhaps a quarter-hour on his ride, would let him overtake Renee, and as he went along it he saw that only one set of tracks showed against the otherwise unbroken expanse of snow. He followed those tracks now, holding the horse to a steady trot.

He had topped the first rise in a series of low hills and the trail was gently dropping toward a sweep of low ground when abruptly, glancing ahead, he saw a pair of riders perhaps a quarter-mile distant. The two were holding their mounts at a stand and facing away from him.

The way in which one man sat the saddle with body cocked and his weight in one stirrup made Phil tighten rein. He knew that this man was Evan Rue even before he recognized the Crow Track animal Rue had ridden out the street earlier. And just as surely did he recognize the short-coupled bay standing alongside Rue.

He had jerked his horse around and headed back up the trail even before he had convinced himself beyond all doubt that the bay's rider was Lew Neal, his father's foreman.

Anger was boiling in him as he topped the crest of the hill and rode out of sight of the pair. Glancing quickly about, he put his animal down the slope and in behind a stunted cedar. From there he could see Rue and Neal.

He watched them for nearly ten minutes, until abruptly Neal rode on out the trail while Rue angled off to the north. By that time his face had gone pale before the rage that was in him. He had witnessed something he scarcely yet believed, a betrayal nothing but his own eyes could have convinced him was even within the realm of possibility.

Shortly before Phil Gardies came upon them there along the trail, Neal had listened to Rue's acid recounting of what had happened to Shep Nye this morning, afterward dryly commenting, "Twice ought to be enough, Ev. Why not forget Harbour?"

Rue caught himself staring at the stiffened middle finger of his right hand, at the white scar across the broken knuckle left by Harbour's bullet. "One day his luck'll run out," he stated. Then, eyeing Neal obliquely, he asked, "Any chance he'll take Gardies' offer?"

"Not from the way the old man talked this morning."

"You're going to have to keep me posted on this, Lew. And on anything else that develops."

"I been going to mention that." . . . Neal appeared worried . . . "Like meetin' you here right now. I had the devil's own time getting away. Let anyone spot me around Crow Track and I could lose my job. This is all a damn' sight riskier than what you and me have been mixed up in till now. Running into you in town now and then like by accident was different."

"I know. But you can come to the layout at night. I sleep in that end room. All you've got to do is ride to the edge of the clearing and rap on my window."

The Bit man shook his head. "I don't like it. You got dogs around the place."

"Only two. They're most nights in the bunkhouse with the boys. No one pays 'em any attention. Now come on, don't be so spooky."

Neal finally nodded in a grudging way. "All right, I'll be across if anything changes." He thought of something then that made him frown and ask, "What happens to this other from now on? Even if I can rig things for you the way I have before, how can you come along and drive off a bunch of our critters any more? You'll have these homesteaders strung out across all that north country."

"They'll be told not to be curious about what they see or hear on certain nights." Sensing Neal's hesitation and reluctance in this matter, Rue added, "Just don't worry. Put the extra dollars in your pocket and let me do the worryin'."

"Let the boss hear what you're doing and he's going to have me put extra men up to the north to keep an eye out. First off, he'll want a couple of men to hang out at our Salt Flats camp. Then —"

"You don't have any Salt Flats camp any more," Rue put in. "Dooley's filed on it by now. He moves in tomorrow."

Neal's weather-burned face went loose with amazement. "Dooley homesteading the Salt Flats? Why, we been using that since long before I signed on with Gardies."

"He don't own it, Lew," the Crow Track man said mildly. "The same goes for the Burnt Hills cabin. Ames goes in there. Randolph and Hawley will be off to the east of him. Then Burke takes his wife and kids and settles on Owl where the north fork comes in."

Neal swore softly, vehemently. "Lord, Ev, you can't make all that stick."

"Let Gardies try to stop us and Bill Parks'll throw the book at him. The old rooster's going to have to string wire if he gets to thinking we can't run our steers right alongside Bit's."

"You think he'll spend three or four thousand putting in fence?"

"Either that or we share all that grass with him."

Bit's foreman shook his head in bewilderment. "It's goin' to be one sweet mess."

"Only if Gardies throws his weight around. I almost hope he will."

"And these Texas cattle come in when?"

"I take the money to Pierce across in Bend in the morning. He guarantees delivery. So it ought to be in three days' time."

Neal breathed in a long sigh, let it go explosively. "So I'm in the middle. Gardies'll want me to put a stop to this. He'll have me put a night crew out first thing."

"You know how to handle that kind of deal, Lew," Rue told him. "Most nights it won't matter where your men are. On the nights when it counts, you send 'em off on a ride toward Owl when we're moving a bunch off that east range. Or if we've got a jag of stuff spotted to the west, you can send your boys the other way on a prowl."

Lew Neal shrugged, finally resigning himself to what he saw coming. "Well, we can give it a try. But go slow and easy on my end of it. Awful slow and awful easy."

"That's what I figured to do. Easy for say a month while everyone gets settled in. Then if a good storm comes along we can get to work again, you and me."

Rue judged he had carried his point, that Neal would think all this over and forget his qualms. And now he told the Bit man, "Remember, you're to let me know if Gardies is up to something."

"Guess I can do that," Neal agreed. "Anything more?"

"Not a thing, Lew. See you in church." Lifting a hand in a parting gesture, Rue put his animal off the trail and toward the nearest rise to the north.

Harry Talbot and Sheriff Parks left Doc Emery's house shortly after the noon hour. As they turned up the street the law man said, "Shep couldn't look worse if he'd stuck his head in a thresher. How did it happen, when Harbour was hardly marked?"

"Search me," Talbot replied. "First it looked like Shep had him dead to rights. Then all of a sudden he didn't. There at the end Harbour could've broke both his arms and his legs if he'd wanted."

"Rue ought to forget his grudge against that man. Tell him I told you that, Harry."

"I will, but it won't do no good."

"Rue needs friends now, not enemies. If he crowds Harbour too far, he could lose everything he's set to gain."

Talbot had nothing to say to this and they continued up the walk in silence until they were opposite the courthouse. Parks said, "So long," cutting across the street to his office while Talbot went on up to the *Niagara* to get his mare and Nye's dun.

Nye came out of Emery's house as Talbot rode down the street leading the dun several minutes later. The big man's stride was unsteady, although when Talbot asked, "Need any help?" he answered thickly, querulously, "I'm walkin', ain't I?"

"You are but you got no right to be."

Talbot watched his fellow crewman manage somehow to pull himself up into the saddle, and afterward they went out the foot of the street at a steady jog. Nye had refused to let Emery bandage his face. It was badly swollen, so puffed that cheek and neck joined in one straight line. Harbour's fists had cut him badly about the mouth and one eye was swollen tight shut. The doctor had been forced to pull the stub of a broken tooth which, along with another Nye had spit out on regaining consciousness, made him slur his words when he presently stated, "I'll get the lanky devil if it takes ten years. I'll lick him first, then take a bull whip to skin him with."

"Me, I'd stay clear of him," Talbot observed.

It was several more minutes before Nye spoke again, this time asking in a subdued way, "Just how could he do that to me? Here I even had him down once. Twice I hit him hard enough to bust his head loose from his shoulders."

"Guess he just don't bust that easy, Shep."

"If I hadn't slipped there that once he'd look like I do now." Nye glanced around, his open eye squinted against the strong sunlight. "I cut him up pretty bad at that, eh?"

"He was hurt some," Talbot said, deciding not to prod the man's unstable temper.

"Bet he was," Nye said, concluding their talk for the next hour and a quarter as they travelled north across the bench, then swung east toward the hills.

It was sight of the Murchison cabin in the distance that finally roused Nye from his aching silence. "Ever hear the likes of the combin' over that old hellion give the boss this morning?"

Talbot grinned on recalling it. "Bet Murch was plenty salty in his day."

"He ain't nothin' to handle now though."

Ten minutes later as they rode in on the homestead, Nye lowered the hand he had been holding against the throbbing left side of his face. His one eye betrayed a look of cunning. "Harry, there's no smoke at the chimney."

Talbot glanced toward the cabin. "It's warmed some. Maybe him and the old woman are doing without a fire."

"Too cold to be without heat." In a few more seconds Nye observed, "Them two nags of his is gone from the corral, Harry."

The other looked around at him in puzzlement. "Suppose they are gone?"

Nye's swollen lips twisted in the semblance of a smile. "You heard how he used his tongue on Evan. You heard him say he'd use buckshot on us."

"Well, so he did. He was riled. I'd of been, too."

"You heard the boss say he was to fence or get out."

"Sure I heard. What you gettin' at?"

They were almost abreast the cabin now, and Nye drawled, "Let's give a look," reining his gelding from the road.

"Look here, Shep. Let's get on."

Talbot's protest had no apparent effect, and he reluctantly followed Nye toward the cabin. By the time he was halfway across the yard, he saw that Nye was coming down out of the saddle and called in rising alarm, "Hey, what you doing?"

Nye ignored him, going to the door and hammering on it so viciously that Talbot spoke again. "Let's be on our way, man. Leave Murch be."

But Nye, facing around, was smiling even more crookedly. "No one home, Harry."

"Then climb back into your hull and let's make tracks."

"Hunh-uh." Nye reached out and tried the door's latch. It lifted easily and he kicked the door open.

"Damn it, what you doing there, Shep?"

"Come along and you'll see."

Nye looked carefully in both directions along the road, then stepped in through the door.

Talbot was about to call out again when he checked himself, knowing that he would be wasting breath, knowing the slow-witted and unforgiving Nye was bound to have his way in this.

He gave a start then as he heard a crash from inside the cabin, and a moment later he was following Nye's example in furtively scanning the road. He wasn't liking this at all as he listened to more sounds of violence issuing from the building. Some heavy object hit the floor with a jolt that shook icicles from the roof's edge. Shortly he heard a clanging of iron followed by the heavy thud of a stove being turned on its side. There was a hollow drumming then as the stove's flue hit the floor.

There came the clatter of dishes being smashed, of pans hitting the floor. Somewhere out back a window burst with a jangling of glass, and it was then that Talbot called stridently, "Shep, get out of here."

He listened to further noises for another quarter-minute, until Nye abruptly appeared in the doorway, his thick chest heaving from his labors. He held a double-bitted axe, and now he eyed Talbot quizzically to ask, "Anyone coming?"

"No, but —"

Nye turned at Talbot's first word, swinging the axe at the door's hinges. He was oblivious to Talbot's shouting until the door finally sagged and fell to the floor inside, its bottom corner wedged against the doorframe by a bent hinge.

Nye stepped back, breathing hard, and looked again along the road. He said then, "Be back in a minute, Harry," and disappeared once more before Talbot could protest.

This time Talbot could hear nothing from inside the building. He was becoming even more worried than before when suddenly Nye was back again, the axe still in hand. Nye's one good eye shone with a look of gloating then as he stepped out from the door and hurled the axe through the one front window. He was laughing crazily as he walked out to the dun and made his awkward climb to the saddle.

Perspiration beaded Harry Talbot's forehead now as they started away, angling back to the road. It didn't calm him in the slightest when Nye told him, "If the boss pays Murch what he said he would, he's *loco*. The place ain't worth fifty dollars as she stands. In another hour it won't be worth even one dollar."

A sudden foreboding gripped Talbot. "What else did you do?"

"Something that'll pay off about the time you and me are getting home, Harry," came Nye's smug reply.

"Something like what?"

Nye's smile broadened. "One of the parlor lamps busted and spilled over the rug. I found me the stub of a candle back in the kitchen. Stuck it to the rug and left it burning. It'll take maybe an hour to touch the place off."

Harry Talbot jerked rein so hard that his animal reared. It took a lot to rouse him, but he was furious now.

Nye, looking around, asked blandly, "What's your trouble, Harry?"

"I'm going back."

"What for?"

"You knot-headed devil. If the boss had wanted Murch burned out he'd have said so."

"He sent me across to put the match to Harbour's layout, didn't he? Murch is as much in our way as Harbour."

"Makes no difference." Talbot started back along the road. "He didn't say it was to happen here."

"Harry."

Talbot glanced around. He saw the gun in Shep Nye's hand. The weapon's bore was lined squarely at him.

"Now you be good and come along home, Harry," Nye told him.

The mid-afternoon sun was bright and warm. Its glare, reflected by the unbroken expanse of fast melting snow, was so blinding that Jim Harbour pulled his wide hat low and tilted his head against it as his black jogged steadily out the north road.

During the first hour of his ride he was aware of little more than the steady hoof falls of the gelding as he thought back over the morning, particularly on what Phil Gardies had told him. Rue's move of bringing in cattle and making his try at cutting into Bit's vast holdings came as even more of a surprise than Nye's attempt at burning him out last night. For he had expected Evan Rue eventually to try and even the score with him whereas he hadn't expected the man to move against Bit so soon, despite Raoul Gardies being crippled.

There in the saloon office this morning after the fight, and as Wickwire was bandaging his arm, he had told the man, "George, I'll take your offer on those warrants. On enough to cover a section."

The gambler had been pleased, but had insisted, "Better take more, Jim."

"No. The interest on even that much will run close to fifty dollars a year. Besides, a section added to what I have now will be all I'll ever need."

So it had been decided that way. He had signed a note agreeing to pay Wickwire five percent interest each year on the value of the warrants to cover a section of land, the price of the warrants to be a dollar and thirty-five cents for each acre.

Later, after his talk with Phil Gardies on the street, he had gone to the Land Office in the courthouse, surrendered the warrants and applied for a government patent on a full section of land. According to the chart the agent showed him, this section along with his present quarter-section would take in most of the grass meadows along that promontory of the hills jutting into the range between Crow Track and Cow Springs.

There had been a fee to pay, and he'd gone to the bank to get the money to cover it. The matter finally settled, he had experienced a satisfaction almost as strong as the one he'd felt the afternoon almost a month ago when he had nailed down the last cedar shake shingle on his cabin roof. And along with this there was a strange gratefulness toward George Wickwire. The man's generosity had been unexpected, genuine. Some day he would find a way of repaying the gambler.

He was thinking all this as he went on along the bench road. During that hour's interval he was stirred from his preoccupation only once, this when the gelding took him straight on north toward Bit and beyond the forks that led eastward to the pass. Turning the black, he put such a hard pressure on the reins that his gashed arm stung for several minutes after he had reached the road that would take him home.

Much later and several miles further on as he was again riding with his head down, a muted sound much like the echo of a strong gust roaring along a timbered slope rode in over his animal's hoof strikes and the creak of leather to rouse him from his indrawn mood a second time. He lifted his head and lazily scanned the road ahead. There, not four hundred yards away, Murchison's cabin patterned a torch of smoke and flame against the dark background of the hills.

He was staggered by what he saw. When he came within fifty yards of the blazing building, when he could feel its heat stronger than that of a summer sun off a desert, he pulled the nervous black to a stand.

No one was in sight, the gate of the corral beyond the cabin stood open. A smaller building he supposed must be a wood shed burned as fiercely as the cabin. Crowding back the futile thought that he should be doing something to save at least a piece of furniture for Murchison, Jim sat numbly watching. He presently noticed the broken window, the sagging door and its splintered frame, all mute testimony to this having been no accident.

In another few seconds the cabin's ridge beam burned through and the roof suddenly collapsed with a rumble that sent flames swirling fifty feet skyward. And the mounting roar of the inferno finally beat so savagely at his brain that he turned the gelding away.

He circled the building, a tight fury in him. He saw that the kitchen window had been broken, that the back door's upper panel had been smashed with an axe. He could look through the opening and see an overturned stove inside and a broken chair. That moment the walls of the shed behind the cabin abruptly caved in, sending out such a blast of heat that he moved away toward the corral.

Having wondered where Murchison and his wife might be, he now found a partial answer as he came upon a set of wheel tracks leading from the corral into the northwest. Bit lay in that direction and he guessed that the homesteader and his wife must have driven across to call on Raoul Gardies. Though Murchison had never been very friendly or neighborly, he decided now that he was obligated to find the man and tell him what had happened.

As he put the black on along the ruts lined out across the snow, he was convinced of something Raoul and Phil Gardies, the attempted firing of his cabin, and even Rue's plan of bringing in the cattle, had failed utterly in making him comprehend. The scene of wanton destruction back there made him wonder now how he could have been so mistaken in his judgment of Evan Rue.

The wrecking and the burning of Murchison's cabin was almost certainly the work of Crow Track. Until ten minutes ago he had judged Rue to be a cautious man who would never over-play his hand despite his plan for throwing cattle onto what had always been considered Bit graze. He had evidently been wrong in this, and his error in foreseeing Rue's intentions made him doubt himself and wonder what element in this gathering trouble he had overlooked.

That doubt and puzzlement stayed with him over the seven miles that finally took him around the margin of a low, rocky butte and brought him within sight of Bit. He had never before seen Raoul Gardies' headquarters and now the sight of it jolted him with a strong wonder.

Lying out from a sheer-walled pocket of the tablelike formation was what at first appeared to be a small town. Three large barns with fenced fields ranging behind them flanked a road striking in from the southwest past a small willow-fringed lake. Lesser buildings were ranked along the road that ended near a maze of corrals and pens deep in the indentation of the hill. A big and rambling log house lay on open ground several hundred yards to the west of the working buildings, a branch road running to it between the fields. Orchard and shade trees grew around the house, giving it a pleasant setting even in this leafless season.

Jim Harbour had seen many big outfits, had worked for several. But he had never before known one that matched Bit either in size or orderliness of layout. And the thought involuntarily struck him, *No wonder he doesn't want to see any of it go.*

He angled across to follow the house track around a pasture and then rode for almost a mile between fenced fields showing the green of winter wheat and new alfalfa in the patches where the wind and the thaw had thinned the snow. He at length came in on a high rock wall enclosing the eastern margin of the house yard. Two saddled horses, a bay and a sorrel, stood hip-shot and drowsing at a rail running along the wall. He turned the black in beyond them, got down and tied.

Taking a brick path footing the wall, he climbed a flight of flagstone steps to a cleared walk. His first glance along the walk brought him a strong surprise at discovering Lew Neal and Renee Gardies standing some thirty feet away near a door at the end of the building.

The girl's back was to him and in the brief moment before Neal saw him he was finding a sharp contrast between what the girl was wearing and her finery of this morning and yesterday. She had on a pair of waist-overalls, scuffed boots and a short wool coat of the same common variety as his own. Had she not been hatless, her ebony hair pulled back and tied with a bright green ribbon, Jim might have supposed that Neal was talking to one of his crew.

Bit's foreman saw him now, said something to Renee. She turned sharply, staring in open amazement as Jim walked in on them taking off his hat.

He nodded, got a cool nod in return from Neal as he was once again feeling the sharp impact of the girl's striking good looks. He asked, "Are the Murchisons around?"

Renee gave him a wondering look, as though this wasn't what she had expected him to say. "They were," she told him. "They left half an hour ago for town."

With a slow sigh, Jim shook his head. "Hate to tell you this, but they're due for a surprise when they get home. I've just come from watching the place burn down."

"You've what?" Neal snapped.

"Burn?" Renee's eyes were staring with shock and incredulity. She breathed in a hurt, stunned way. "Oh, no."

Jim nodded soberly. "It's gone by now. From what I could make out, whoever did it smashed up the cabin before touching it off."

"Who'd pull a low trick like that on Tom and Carrie?" Neal flared.

"Anybody's guess. I couldn't lift a hand. By the time I got there it would have cooked a man to go near the place."

"But what's to happen to them?" The girl spoke in a hushed, dazed tone. "I'll have to get word to them, tell them to come back here and stay." She glanced helplessly at Bit's foreman. "Maybe Phil could do that, Neal."

He nodded. "Him or me, doesn't matter. What'll I tell him on what we were just talking about, where he's to bed down?"

Renee lifted a hand to her forehead, rubbing it as though trying to steady her confused thoughts. "It had better be down in the bunkhouse. Dad nearly had a stroke when I told him Phil was coming out to stay for good."

She eyed Jim once more, aloofly, almost in unfriendliness. "Thank you for coming, Harbour. Even if it was only to find Murchison." Over the barest pause, she added, "For a moment I thought you were here to take the job."

Jim was taken aback by her frankness and glanced uneasily at Neal. She saw that and told him, "You needn't be afraid to talk about it. Dad told Neal after he got home from seeing you two nights ago."

Jim lifted his wide shoulders, let them fall, saying nothing. The gesture seemed to irritate her, for as she spoke now there was a caustic quality in her tone. "You still can't see it? Not even after this, after Rue burning Tom and Carrie out?"

Before Jim could answer, Neal was saying, "I wouldn't go as far as claimin' that just yet, miss."

"You wouldn't?" She swung angrily around on him. "Then just who do you think did it?"

The Bit foreman's face took on color. And Jim was feeling out of place, wanting to get away. But there was another thing he had wanted to mention and now he asked, "Any chance of seeing your father, Miss Gardies?"

Renee's glance came around to him again. "I suppose so, if it's necessary. He's taking a nap."

"It's not that important," Jim was quick to say. "Might as well tell you as him. It's just something I got to thinking about on the way across here."

When she didn't speak, only gave him a questioning look, he asked, "Have you heard what friend Rue plans to do?"

"Buy those Texas cattle and bring them in?" She caught his nod, said, "Yes, Phil and I heard about it this morning in town."

Jim deliberated a moment before telling her. "The way I understand it, Rue takes half the money across to Pierce in Bend tomorrow to wind up the deal. What I got to wondering is what Pierce would do if someone besides Rue got to him first. With all the money instead of half."

Renee's look was momentarily puzzled. But then her brows arched in strong surprise. "You mean . . . dad should buy the herd instead of Rue?"

"It'd be a sure way of cutting the props from under the man."

Suddenly Renee was smiling at him in a warm and genuinely friendly way. Until now her tone and manner toward him had been distant, strictly neutral. It had been as though, having judged him yesterday, she had found nothing over these past few minutes to cause her to revise that judgment.

Yet now she made it plain that she was revising it. "This may be the chance dad's been waiting for, Harbour." A wondering quality was in her eyes. "How nice of you to do this. But why are you doing it?"

"Maybe because I'm selfish. Because you're helping me if you keep Rue in line."

Giving him another fleeting smile that betrayed a new awareness of him, she turned toward the door. "Dad will want to talk to you about this. Neal, take Harbour around to the porch."

As she went into the house, Neal said gruffly, "This way," giving Jim an unfriendly scowl as he started off across the snow and around the front corner of the house. Jim could sense the man's hostility as they walked on along the front of the long building toward a vine-bordered porch midway the length of its wall of square-hewn logs.

They were sauntering in on the porch steps when they heard a door slam. Jim glanced above to see Renee come to the porch's edge.

Her eyes were staring at him with shock and alarm. Her face had lost its high coloring. She looked down at them in a frantic, numb way.

"You'd better come in, both of you," she said unsteadily. "I . . . I think my father's dead."

Chapter 4

Raoul Gardies was dead.

Jim Harbour reached for a blanket lying over the back of the horsehair sofa, unfolded it and laid it gently over the old man's body, drawing it up over the grey head. Then, looking up at Lew Neal who had been standing helplessly by, he nodded toward the porch door, saying quietly, "Better go get Phil."

Neal turned away at once, obviously relieved to be leaving, and the soft closing of the door behind Bit's foreman made Jim hard aware of being alone with Renee Gardies. He felt inadequate and awkward. Having so far avoided looking at the girl, he did so now to find her staring at her father's blanket-draped shape in a dazed, lost way.

"I'm sorry it had to happen, Miss Gardies. Is there anything you'd like me to do? Take the word to town, anything else?"

Renee shook her head tiredly, her eyes coming around to him in a vacant stare, as though she had forgotten his being here. "Thank you, no. Phil's here. And Neal." Then she was once again glancing at the sofa, saying in a low voice, "He looked so . . . so at peace. It couldn't have been hard for him, could it?"

"Hardly. He probably never knew it was happening."

She lifted a hand and ran it across her forehead. "I suppose the tears will come later." . . . She gave Jim a troubled, beseeching look . . . "Just now it's hard to believe."

Five minutes ago on hurrying in here Jim had tossed his hat to the floor. He stepped over now and stooped to pick it up, asking, "Would you like me to stay till Neal gets back?"

"No. No, I'm perfectly all right."

He crossed the end of the room as unobtrusively as he could and was reaching out to open the door when Renee abruptly said, "I think I'll come with you," speaking hurriedly, as though unable to face the prospect of being alone.

They walked out onto the porch and were going down the steps when she spoke in a barely audible voice. "He was a good man, Jim Harbour. Better than you know. Sometimes it seemed that he was too good, that he tried too hard to do what he believed was right. It's hard to realize how few people understood him, how many he hurt."

"Isn't it like that with most of us, miss?

When they tally the good in me against the bad, the good'll be mighty shy."

She hesitated at the foot of the steps but then finally stepped down into the snow to walk beside him toward the corner of the house. "What's to happen to all this?" she asked in a wondering way, gesturing toward the working buildings of the ranch in the distance. "Dad mentioned something you said to him the other night. I think how he put it was that you said you wouldn't care if the pack jumped Bit and tore it apart."

She wasn't looking at him, didn't see the flush of embarrassment that darkened his flat-planed cheeks as she went on, "There must be a lot of others who think as you do. Now that dad's gone they really will try and tear us apart, won't they?"

"You shouldn't be thinking about such things right now, miss."

" 'Miss,' " she echoed dryly. But then, evidently thinking she might have offended, she said quickly, "From now on you're to call me Renee. It . . . the other makes it sound as though we're complete strangers. And we're not. Not after this."

"No, not quite."

In another moment she said, "I should be thinking of what to do. Thinking of it now, before it's too late."

Her voice trembled and he was uneasily aware of her putting a handkerchief to her eyes. Pretending he hadn't noticed, he told her, "Let Phil do the worrying. Running this outfit is a man's chore."

"I'll not see it happen. I'll keep it from happening."

She had control of her emotions once again and now he gave her a quick glance, seeing that her eyes were shining with tears but that she was aroused, angry. "You'll keep what from happening?"

"The pack won't tear Bit apart. I'll do what you said, buy those cattle Rue's after. I'm going to handle that man the way dad would have handled him." . . . She looked around, meeting his glance . . . "Do you really think Pierce would sell to us rather than to Rue?"

Jim shrugged. "He must be after the best deal he can get. He wouldn't be likely to turn down the chance of getting all his money right away instead of half now and the other half next year. Especially if you paid him more than Rue's offering. I'd go as high as five thousand, which is a good price for you."

"Then Phil's going across to Bend with the money tonight, before Rue has the chance to get to him." . . . She gave Jim a look of gratefulness. . . . "Phil will be wanting to thank you for this. It may make a lot of difference in what's to happen."

"May make no difference at all in how things wind up, though. Rue isn't the man to give in because he stubs his toe once. If this doesn't work he'll try something else."

They walked on in silence for several seconds, Jim feeling a strong admiration for this girl. He could sense how she was struggling not to show her grief and knew that her fierce pride and loyalty to her father was responsible for her talking this way.

And now she looked up at him to ask soberly, "What would you do if you were running Bit from now on? How would you deal with Rue and these others?"

They were coming in on the walk, approaching the steps leading from the yard. Jim slowed his pace. "Putting yourself in another man's place isn't easy."

"I know. But exactly how would you go about it?"

"If you'd asked me two hours ago, before I saw what happened to Murchison, answering that would have been easy."

"How would you have answered it?"

"I'm on the other side of the fence, always have been," he bluntly told her. "Because I am, I'd have said you should give people like Pete Hapgood and Bailey and one or two others their chance. By letting them move their families in to settle off there on the good side of Owl. Maybe as far east as Porcupine. There aren't many of them really serious about proving up on a homestead and they wouldn't put a dent in your range. If you satisfied them, gave them more than they'd ever hoped for, you'd have Rue all on his own."

He halted now as they came to the head of the steps. Renee regarded him speculatively a long moment. "This is probably what you'd have told me yesterday if I'd given you the chance." Giving him a brief smile, she said, "So that would have been your answer two hours ago. What would your answer be now?"

"Look, Renee," he protested. Then, made ill at ease by having involuntarily called her by name, he hurried on to say, "What you'd do and what I would are two different things. But after what I saw this afternoon I wouldn't back off to Rue or anyone else. Not even to the one or two good men who've gone into this cattle deal with him. If any one of them steps outside the law as Rue did in burning out Murchison, they're all to blame."

Her green eyes were alive with interest now. "What do you mean by not backing off?"

"That'd depend on friend Rue's next move," he answered. "But right now you could begin whittling him down to size by moving two or three hundred head of cattle onto that east range before he can move any of his onto it. You could move a crew of men across to Murchison's place even if they had to live in a tent all winter. These critters Rue's buying are in poor shape. They couldn't stand a winter on a crowded range. If Rue objected and started something, you could —"

"But if we bought those cattle before he could, we'd have stopped him even before he could start anything, wouldn't we?"

Jim nodded. "For right now, yes. But can you lay hands on five thousand dollars on such short notice? It's a little late in the day."

"Phil can go in and have Baker go back to the bank and get him the money." She was studying him closely, and now, smiling mischievously, she said, "There's a bruise on the side of your face, Jim. Did Nye put it there or did I?"

His hand lifted to his cheek. He couldn't hold back a broad grin. "You pack quite a wallop, but Nye gets the credit for this."

"I wish now I hadn't lost my temper."

She was serious once again and, matching her mood, he soberly told her, "Shouldn't have said what I did." Then turning down the steps, he added, "Call on me if I can help in any way."

Renee nodded. "You won't change your mind about taking the job?"

"There's no need now. Phil's with you and if he can buy those cattle the chances are things'll simmer down."

She gave him a skeptical look. "I suppose it won't hurt to hope you're right. But I don't really believe you are."

It was a rare evening when George Wickwire could be found in the *Niagara* between the hours of eight and nine, and had been for two months now since the night on which some unknown man had molested Hester Britt on her way home from the stage office and stolen her purse. Tonight the gambler followed his usual practice and left the saloon at five minutes before eight, going briskly along the shadowed walk toward the street intersection four doors below the saloon.

He had let it be known that this brief respite from the day's routine of working in his office and playing cards constituted his only form of recreation. And, after these many nights of spending sometimes as long as half an hour striding the streets in both good and bad weather, he had finally overcome a natural distaste for any form of exercise and arrived at the point of actually looking forward to his nightly walk, having found it invigorating and in other ways rewarding.

He had, for instance, discovered that absent-minded old Franz Ulrich would often leave his harness and saddle shop without locking the door. Wickwire made it a point of always passing the shop and, if he found the door open, of locking it and leaving the key with the saloon swamper for Ulrich to collect the following morning.

Among other things, he had become distantly acquainted with certain people he seldom saw on Alder's street during the daylight hours. One of these was a stooped and shrivelled old woman who prowled the streets and the alleys pulling a packing crate to which were fixed the wheels of a baby buggy. The box received a variety of such odds and ends as pieces of coal and wood, discarded burlap sacks and empty bottles. The old woman smoked a cob pipe. On many nights it was filled with the tobacco she had shredded from the generous stub of one of Wickwire's carefully discarded cheroots.

Another thing the gambler had discovered was that Judge Bullock, widowed and turning deaf with his advancing years, rarely drew the shade on his first-floor bedroom window. On occasion a group of youngsters would be across the street from the house giggling and watching the eminent jurist undress, scratch himself luxuriously and then climb into bed clad in his long woolen underwear before blowing out his lamp.

Wickwire had also learned that Hester Britt was quite punctual about closing the office shack at the stage yard at eight o'clock and then walking to her home far out at the lower end of the street.

At that hour the saloonman would invariably be either within sight of the stage office or close enough to the intersection to see the girl when she rounded the hotel corner from Cedar Street into Main. He would then unobtrusively follow her out Main to her house at the edge of town, most often taking the path across the street and keeping well behind her.

Not once in the weeks since starting his evening constitutional because of Hester had he spoken to her or, in fact, even once encountered her face to face. Never having met her formally, it nonetheless seemed that he knew Hester Britt well. He could recognize her small, slender shape at a distance. He could identify her quick and purposeful step even at a distance if he heard it sounding against the planks of a walk or the cinders of the lower street path.

He even knew her face well, though he had only once had the chance of studying it closely, that occasion being some three months ago when he had gone to the stage yard to pay his fare for a trip out to Denver. This one brief experience in proximity to the girl had left her image sharply graven on his memory. He remembered quite clearly each detail of feature, her serene and proud look that betrayed nothing of the disappointment and heartache that seemed to be her destiny in having married Ben Britt. He knew that her cheeks and uptilted nose were heavily freckled. He was certain that the curl of her sandy hair had never needed the encouragement of an iron. And he also guessed that the fine needlework of her shirtwaists and the fashionable cut of her one coat were of her own doing.

Ben Britt should have been proud of his wife. If he was no one in town had ever learned of it. Nor did his known susceptibility to other women indicate it. For four years now Hester Britt had collected the fares, kept the ledgers, hired and fired the yard hostlers, bought and traded the animals and made the excuses for non-payment of bills that had kept Ben Britt's stage business alive. Wickwire could only imagine what the struggle was costing Hester, for Ben seldom helped at either office or yard when he was in town. And never once had Wickwire seen the man accompany his wife on her solitary night walks from the office to their house at the town's outskirts.

Once, six weeks ago on a night when Ben had been drinking earlier at the *Niagara*, the gambler had seen the door of the Britt house close on Hester and had turned back toward the center of town only to be stopped by hearing a woman scream. He had wheeled about in time to see Hester run from the porch and across the yard to stand warily beyond the fence watching the open door. Wickwire had been about to walk over to her when, hesitantly, she had gone back into the house. He had stayed there in the deep shadows across the street watching and listening until, half an hour later, the lamplight faded from the parlor window.

If George Wickwire had been asked to explain his nightly routine of escorting Hester Britt from a distance, of watching over her, he would have been hard put for an answer. He might have given the reason that this lone girl had already been once molested on her solitary way along the dark street. He might have mentioned the fact of it being generally known that she carried the day's proceeds of the office in her purse, and that it had once been stolen.

His agile brain might have invented any one of a number of plausible answers far afield from the truth, which was that he found Hester Britt exceedingly attractive, that he had found in her a kindred solitary and lonely spirit, and finally that he pitied her because she had married a worthless man. He would have been incensed had someone reminded him that Hester Britt's affairs were her own and no concern of his.

Tonight Hester was late. The stage office window was still lighted when Wickwire passed it for the second time five minutes after the courthouse bell had tolled its eight strokes. He went on out Main Street and past the last store before turning back, expecting to see her familiar shape outlined against the lamplight shining from the hotel's glassed veranda at the intersection.

But the walk was empty. Vaguely disappointed and a little concerned, he pulled the fur collar of his coat tighter to his neck against the bite of the chill air and retraced his steps. He was within a stride or two of the joining of the cross street walks when suddenly she came around the corner of the hotel porch, almost colliding with him.

He instinctively reached out to catch her. And when she laughed, stepping aside as his hands brushed her and saying in confusion, "That was almost an accident," he smiled and tipped his hat, answering, "Could've been serious. Good evening, Mrs. Britt."

She nodded pleasantly. He had stepped on past her when she suddenly startled him by speaking again. "Mr. Wickwire. Can you . . . do you have a moment?"

Wickwire turned. "Indeed. More than a moment if you'd like."

She looked up at him uncertainly, embarrassment ridding her face of its plainness and making her quite pretty as her cheeks took on color. "I shouldn't be doing this," she said in a low voice, "but . . ." She motioned down the street. "Would you mind going a little way with me?"

"Mind? It would be a pleasure, ma'am."

They started down the walk an arm-length apart, and she waited until they were in the shadows beyond the hotel lights before telling him, "It's about Ben. Or I should say it's about yesterday morning. About the accident. You must have heard about it."

"Yes."

"We're sorry to have put Miss Gardies out. I intend apologizing to her."

"She evidently understood it couldn't be helped."

"But it could have been helped." She turned to look at him directly. "Ben had been drinking, hadn't he?"

"Not so far as I've heard," he lied.

He caught her sigh of relief. "You would certainly have heard if he had been. What you say makes it easier to take."

"Makes what easier, Mrs. Britt?"

"I've been going over the accounts tonight." She smiled in a way that was both proud and regretful. "It . . . they make it look like we're finished."

The gambler sharply slowed his stride, feeling something tighten in him. "That can hardly be."

"But it is," she murmured. "Ben went up there this morning to see how much damage had been done. It was an old coach. Both axles are broken, one side's smashed, two wheels are gone. And it needs a new thoroughbrace. It wouldn't pay us to rebuild it."

Wickwire sauntered along deep in thought, shortly asking, "Can't you pick up another somewhere at a fair price?"

"Perhaps. Majors across at Bear Creek has an old Barlow-Sanderson. But it's only a mud wagon, not fit for winter driving. He's been using it to haul feed." She shrugged, adding, "So we're left with but one stage, which means we give up either the north or south run. We gave up the south one today."

"Are you having me understand that this means the difference between keeping on or closing the yard?"

She soberly considered his question, at length looking up and giving him a slow nod. "It's almost that. Halfway, let's say. The other half is Ben and his drinking, which you know about too well."

He sighed gustily. "I sometimes wonder at the business I'm in." There was an edge of bitterness to his tone. "Circumstances sometimes force a man into something that shames him if he lets himself think. My mother has doubtless turned many a time in her grave. She didn't bear a son to become a tinhorn and whiskey peddler."

Straightening his shoulders and smiling down at her, he said, "But enough of the confessional. If you say the word I'll see to it that Ben never buys another drink at the *Niagara*."

"If I thought that would stop him I'd have asked you long ago to do just that," she said quietly. "But there are other places in Alder that sell whiskey. And if they agreed not to let him have any he'd freight it in by the barrel and drink in my kitchen."

"You know him better than I."

"Don't misunderstand me," she flared. "Ben's good. He's a fine man most of the time. But he isn't like he was a few years ago, happy go lucky and never worrying. Somehow he's got started wrong here. We've been in debt, which is why I think he drinks. I keep thinking if we could get away somewhere he could get a job and straighten out. He's a fine teamster. He could make forty dollars a week in California, even more in Virginia City."

"Would it be any different than here, Mrs. Britt?"

"It might be. He might settle down and do the things I want to do. If he was working at good wages I could stay home and keep house. And we could have children. Living the way we do here, with me working and him gone every other night, he says we don't dare risk raising a family. We barely get along as it is . . ."

Her words broke off, and in another moment she was saying shyly, "I have no right to be talking like this, telling you these things." She laughed nervously, with no amusement whatsoever. "But it struck me back there when I almost bumped into you that . . . that you're not exactly a stranger. Even though we've met only that once when you came to the office. I sometimes see you walking at night and . . . well, I've heard good things about you. Even so, right now it seems that I don't really know you well enough to ask what I was going to."

"Suppose you pretend we're good friends

and ask it anyway. What can I do to help?"

Over a moment's silence, she said, "You must understand one thing, Mr. Wickwire. I wouldn't be doing this unless . . . unless Ben and I were in real trouble."

"I do understand."

They walked on for several seconds until he wondered if she was going to speak, until she abruptly told him, "I've been to the bank today. I've offered Mr. Baker the business along with the house if he would give me as little as five hundred dollars, enough to take us out of here. He wasn't interested."

Pausing, she went on in a firmer voice, "Meeting you just now I was thinking of all the people you must know. I'd hoped you could suggest someone I could go to. Someone who'd be interested in buying us out. It's a good business, especially with the railroad making the run up here from Bend only twice each week. A man with just a little more than we have could make a really good thing of the start we've got. But we've never been able to do more than just get along from day to day."

Something in George Wickwire, an indefinable hope perhaps, died that moment. Then, not wanting to say it, he nevertheless told her, "There will be five hundred dollars deposited to your name in the bank when it opens in the morning, Mrs. Britt. Consider it done and make your plans accordingly."

Hester Britt halted sharply. Even in this feeble light Wickwire could read the embarrassment written on her face. "I didn't intend that you should take it this way," she said in a cool, proud way. "I was serious when I said I'd hoped you knew someone to send me to. But it never occurred to me to ask for charity, to —"

"My dear woman, I'm a businessman," he cut in. "And a hard man with the dollar. I shall make money on the proposition. I shall also gain something in self respect by banking honest money, as you might guess."

"But you know nothing about the stage business," she protested, warmth coming back into her voice.

"I'll hire someone who does know it. Of course, buying you out at that figure would be taking advantage. I'll find someone to make a fair appraisal and send the balance on to you when it's decided what the price is to be."

"No," she said. "No, I won't have it this way." She was uncertain of herself now and lifted her hands to her temples, lowering her head as though bewildered, as though she was trying desperately not to give in to this strong temptation.

"Look, Mrs. Britt," he drawled patiently. "I had no notion at all that the yard was for sale or I would doubtless have approached you on the matter long before this. The town's growing. I shall make the run to Bend and back all in one day instead of the two days Ben now takes for the trip. Then there's freighting, something you haven't been able to afford but something I can. I'll make money. I'll . . ."

Suddenly she was looking up at him, making him check his words. He caught the shine of tears in her eyes as she reached out and gripped his arms tightly. "You mean it?" she asked, her voice breaking. "You aren't doing this because you're sorry for us? Because you think —"

"Leave my feelings out of this, Mrs. Britt. And yours. Both of us will profit from the arrangement. That's all there is to be said."

"George Wickwire, you . . ."

Her words were choked off by a sob. And then, before he realized what she intended, she came very close to him and lifted her face and kissed him on the cheek.

He was reaching out to take her in his arms when she abruptly turned and ran away along the walk.

A mixture of stubbornness and guile had

dictated Evan Rue's choice of a place to settle when he first came to the bench two years after he had been mustered out of the Union army. Deciding he would run cattle on what he had been told was another man's range, he nevertheless decided not to be too bold about it. He chose an inconspicuous spot backed by hills into which he could retreat if forced by circumstance, locating the working quarters of his ranch in a half-mile-deep bay along the bench's eastern edge.

It was purely by accident that Rue found himself surrounded by such an abundance of nature's bounty. He could look westward from the broad neck of the pocket across a score of miles of lush grass country. It was a sight to stir a cattleman, yet, because he was insensitive to such things and because all that country belonged to Bit, Rue never felt anything but irritation when he gazed in that direction. The foothills lifted tier on tier into the east, finally to merge with the white majesty of the towering Arrowhead peaks. A creek wound lazily across the open ground of Rue's location, which was three-quarters ringed by timber that provided shelter from the winds, good cover for game and an endless supply of firewood and building materials.

Because of Rue's original sense of impermanence in having so brazenly settled where he knew he didn't belong, he built shoddily. He had used aspen logs in place of pine in throwing up his cabin, and for what appeared to him a logical reason. A stand of aspen grew several hundred yards closer to the cabin site than did the sturdier pine, and since he was working alone he calculated he saved perhaps two or three weeks by the substitution.

As a consequence his house now wore a dilapidated, run-down look, as did everything else about the layout. If a corral post rotted through, Rue would have it propped up rather than replace it. If wind tore shingles from a roof, or if a fire burned a hole as it had last winter in the kitchen shanty at one end of the crew cabin, he saw that a patch was made of sheet metal from a discarded washtub, or even from rusted tomato cans, this on the theory that such a makeshift repair was far easier than splitting and curing new shingles. Besides, such measures would last until he acquired more range and could move out onto the bench proper and build permanently.

Tonight, answering the summons of the Chinaman's hammering on the iron wheel-rim outside the kitchen door, Rue had walked down from the house at dusk feeling an unfamiliar sense of buoyancy, of well-being.

After all these years of furtively and jealously eyeing the vast expanse of the bench, he was no longer a mere onlooker. In three more days he was moving out of this timber-constricted stretch of grass and onto open range. He would go as far west as he chose, and all the way south to Cow Springs. He had a tough four-man crew to back his gamble, he had friends. Nothing was going to stop him.

Crow Track's crew quarters was a squat sod-roofed cabin chinked with mud. Four sagging bunks ranged one end of the main room, a long eating table the inner end. A flimsy partition of pine slabs closed off a small cubicle beyond the table, this second room being where George, the Chinese cook, slept alongside his kitchen.

Tonight Rue was genial during the meal, surprising Talbot and Fred Mayes, who joined him for supper. He even managed to make a jocular remark or two at hearing Shep Nye's labored snoring sounding from the far end of the room, though he was careful to avoid any mention of the reasons for the man's indisposition, being sensitive on its causes.

Harry Talbot was unusually glum and silent during the meal, Rue noticed. The man finished eating quickly, announcing as he left the table that he was riding across to the Burnt Hills cabin to see if Bit had yet taken any exception to Ames having moved onto the location.

Rue was only mildly curious as to why Talbot had seemed so preoccupied. "Must have a girl on the string," was Fred Mayes' guess when Rue asked him why Talbot would be riding an unnecessary eight miles at night when he should shortly be thinking of going to bed.

But in another ten minutes when the fourth Crow Track rider, Mose Ehlert, came in off the trail and to the cabin with the news of Murchison's cabin being burned, Rue's naturally suspicious nature gave instant meaning to Talbot's strange behavior.

He wanted to believe that the fire had been an accident, as Mose Ehlert contended. He wanted to believe it even as he got up from the table and went across to shake Nye roughly from his aching and restless dozing.

Nye, either because he wasn't quite awake, or because he didn't care, answered Rue's clipped question with, "So the candle did the trick, eh?"

Rue stood speechless a moment. Then suddenly a blind rage hit him. The two crewmen at the table stiffened as he began cursing Nye apoplectically, obscenely, his voice shortly rising to a hoarse shouting.

Nye was awed and half afraid at first. But

then the insults finally roused him to slow anger, until suddenly he reached in under his mattress and pulled out his Colt's.

He didn't point the gun at Rue. Yet sight of it made the man break off his words. And Nye, mad but nevertheless astonished by what he had done, said in a croaking voice, "That's enough, boss. Keep your tongue off me."

"But why in the name o' God would you do it?"

"Why? Because that busted down old fool hollered at you this mornin' the way you been hollerin' at me just now. Because . . ."

The slam of the door cut across his words. He no longer had an audience. For Rue had abruptly turned and stalked from the room. And now as he stepped outside, feeling the bite of the night's raw air and faintly hearing the voices of Mayes and Ehlert sounding from the cabin, Rue's ire burned itself out enough to let him understand what Shep Nye's stupidity might be costing him.

First, if Crow Track was suspected of having fired Murchison's place, he would probably lose two of the men who had this morning gone with him in his plan for dotting Bit's north range with homesteads. These two, and perhaps one or two others, would have no stomach for being even remotely connected with such an act of outlawry. If they ever discovered the truth of what had happened to Murchison, they would pull out, maybe even leave the country.

More important, if that truth ever became known the bench's tolerance for any wholesale move against Raoul Gardies would be severely strained. Rue's hole card in this gamble had been strict adherence to keeping within the law. Yet today, regardless of his having had no hand in it, he had put himself outside the law. If Crow Track was blamed for Murchison losing his home, Bill Parks was hamstrung even before he had the chance of backing any move against Bit.

Then no one's going to know. Rue tried to convince himself that no one would ever know of what had really happened at Murchison's, yet he couldn't quite believe that. He was feeling cheated, thwarted just now. Twenty minutes ago it had seemed that he had everything well in hand. Now he had the sense of having lost his firm grip on what was to happen.

He was bleakly considering all this as his boots crunched through the crusted snow just short of the shadowy outline of his house. Suddenly, unexpectedly, the night's stillness was rudely broken by a voice saying querulously out of the shadows close ahead,

"You sure took your damn' sweet time gettin' here."

Rue inexplicably felt a moment's stark fear before he recognized Lew Neal's voice. He breathed a sigh of irritation at his nerves being so on edge, saying as he walked toward the man, "Wasn't expecting you. Anything wrong?"

"There is and there isn't," was Neal's answer.

Rue could finally see Neal in the darkness, and as he came up on Bit's foreman he was asked, "Evan, if you could pick the thing you'd like most to happen, what would it be?"

Rue was quick to sense that Neal's reason for being here was important. "Get on with it."

"Then get yourself set for a jolt, friend."

What Rue heard over the next minute worked a vast change in his mood. His depression left him, the news of Raoul Gardies' passing made his pulse pound so savagely in exhilaration that he was short of breath. "It's settled," he breathed. "Nothing can stop us now."

"No? Then wait'll you hear this other." And Neal went on to tell of Phil Gardies' riding across to Bend tonight.

In those few seconds Rue's sureness left him until shortly his black mood was on him once again. Added to that was a new, sharp feeling of urgency that finally made him interrupt the Bit man by snapping, "What time did he leave?"

"Right after five."

"Lord, man, that's over two hours ago. What took you so long getting here?"

"Had to think of a reason for leaving. I'm supposed to be taking the word about the old man to the boys at the ridge camp. But I been waiting here for you a good twenty minutes."

Indecision held Rue only a moment. He said brusquely, "Better clear out, Lew," and ran across and into his cabin.

He wanted to light a lamp, but when the first match broke he tossed it aside and hurried on into his bedroom. He groped for his heavy coat hanging from a hook on the wall by his bed, finally found it and thrust an arm into a sleeve. He spent some seconds rummaging underneath some clothes in the top drawer of his bureau, finally lifting out a salt sack containing the money he had collected at the meeting in Shoemaker's office this morning.

Realizing how little time he had, knowing that Phil Gardies might already be well ahead of him, he hurried so in leaving the cabin that he rammed into a chair near the door, overturning it and hurting his leg. He was mumbling an oath and pulling on his coat then as he rushed out the door and ran for the corral.

Rue would have chosen his favorite grey for this night's long ride. But, the grey having covered the distance to town and back today, he decided on a fresher animal. His ugly temper flared when he had trouble getting a rope on his second choice, a chestnut mare. And he was rough with the animal once he caught her, rough in the way he forced the bit into her mouth and in the way he used a knee against her barrel to pull the cinch tight.

Fred Mayes came sauntering down from the crew cabin as he led the mare from the corral. "Where to, boss?"

"Bend. Look for me back sometime in the morning." Rue climbed into the saddle.

"Thought you was making that trip tomorrow." When he got no reply, the man asked, "Want anyone to go with you?"

"No. You look after things while I'm gone, Fred. And tell Harry he's going to answer to me for something when I get back."

"Answer for what?"

Rue didn't bother explaining, instead threw his spurs viciously into the mare's flank so that she lunged at once into a hard run.

As the animal carried him into the south trail he knew he should be easing her into her night's work rather than wasting her energy this foolishly. But the realization that Phil

Gardies might already be well up the pass road made him throw aside all caution. And presently as he took a little-used side trail leading steeply to a high reach of the pass road he was again using the spur.

He had ridden another half-mile when he began impotently cursing himself for not having taken the long way around. The snow was deep here and lay drifted heavily across the open stretches where the trees thinned. This short-cut was costing him time. It would cost him even more if he turned back. So he kept on, all the while pushing the mare.

The animal was badly blown when, twenty minutes after leaving Crow Track, he came suddenly into the pass road. Common sense finally had its way with him and he grudgingly pulled the mare to a stand. He sat there restlessly trying to listen, an unruly anger holding him as the chestnut's loud heaving kept him from hearing any of the night sounds.

He shortly thought of something that took him from the saddle. Squatting down, he struck a match and held it in his cupped hands, and by its light carefully examined the breadth of the road. He found a variety of tracks and wheel marks and in the end tried to believe that none of them were fresh. It was freezing now, had been since shortly before sundown, and all these markings showed the curled edges that meant they had been left here during the day, during the hours of the thaw.

Rue was somewhat relieved as he went on, and for the first time began thinking of the change Raoul Gardies' dying might bring to his chances for the future. Bit would most certainly not be the power it had been. Phil Gardies made a pale and weak image when compared to his parent. His sister was but a woman, incapable of commanding the respect and awe that had kept Bit intact all these years.

He finally laughed aloud with sheer delight at the prospect he saw before him. Crow Track would grow. He would move out onto the bench proper and build the layout he had dreamed of. Raoul Gardies had set him a good example and he now found that he had every intention of following that example.

Unwittingly, he was pushing the mare too fast again. He had gone barely a mile beyond the point where he had reached this winding, climbing road and his animal was once more laboring, unable to go any faster than a slow jog. So he reluctantly drew rein for the second time and eased back in the saddle to stretch his legs.

For a time he listened to the restless sighing of the gentle breeze through the tops of the nearby spruce sounding in over the chestnut's whistling breathing, to the murmur of a rapids coming from the bed of a stream in the ravine below.

Suddenly, from a lower switch-back of the road, he caught the faintest mutter of a staccato sound. It faded almost immediately, thinned to an echo and was gone. He listened, trying to catch it again. But the slow heaving of the mare was all he could hear.

Impatient, he came down out of the saddle, ground-haltered the animal and walked back along the road some twenty yards until he could no longer hear the mare. He was still walking when the sound reached him once more. This time it was louder.

It was unmistakably the muffled, steady hoof echo of a trotting horse.

A panic hit Rue. He turned and ran clumsily back up the road. He snatched up the mare's reins and was about to climb back into the saddle when, thinking of the winded animal he told himself, *Not a chance.*

If the rider below on the road was Phil Gardies it would be a matter of only a quarter-hour, or even less, before Gardies overtook him. What would happen if they met was something Rue didn't dwell upon, for he quickly decided that if this was Gardies the man was never to suspect that anyone was within miles of him.

Rue thought of the .38 at his hip now. But he ruled out using it, thinking of Neal having ridden across to Crow Track and of Fred Mayes knowing where he was riding tonight. Using a bullet on Gardies, even to wound him, would mean running too much of a risk.

He was standing there alongside the mare, his hand resting on the horn, when he all at once noticed the coiled rope tied to his saddle. And he instantly knew what he would do.

Stepping away and jerking on the reins, he led the mare off the road and up through the trees along the slope immediately beyond. He fought the animal's reluctance to follow, and he was breathing heavily when presently he looked down to see that the road was finally hidden from view. He quickly wound the reins about the wrist-thick branch of a pine and his hands were trembling as he jerked loose the thong that held his rope to the saddle.

The snow was deep here and his stride was awkward as he started wading back down to the road. He paused once, listening, but couldn't catch the sound of the rider below. Concluding that whoever it was must be holding his pony to a walk now, he hurried on.

He lost his footing close above the road, fell and slid downward. He came erect brushing snow from his coat, looking about him. What finally took his eye was a dark smear against the shadowed grey blackness off to his left. He stumbled over to it, giving an explosive sigh of relief at finding it to be the jagged stump of a small tree.

He was tossing the loop of his rope over the stump when he once again heard the animal below along the road. A paralysis held him momentarily at realizing how close the rider must be. But then he wheeled out across the uneven ruts, uncoiling the rope and letting it sag against the frozen mud.

The road fell sharply away beyond the far shoulder. Rue, the hoof falls of the oncoming horse hurrying him, slid down through the snow of the steep shoulder and in behind the thick trunk of a tall aspen. He tried to quiet his labored breathing, hearing the animal above very plainly.

Now was the time to use care. He made sure that the rope was slack even though he held it quarter-circled around the tree's trunk. Looking above then, he saw a shadow move up toward him out of the darkness.

A gusty sigh escaped him as he peered at the man in the saddle, recognizing his shape. Gardies was holding his animal to a brisk trot now and Rue had to act swiftly. He crouched, eyeing the line of the rope going up the bank and across the road.

Gardies' mount was within three feet of the

rope when Rue all at once leaned back, drawing the rope taut around the trunk of the aspen. Then suddenly the rope was almost torn from his grasp, burning his palms as he saw the animal's forelegs buckle. He plainly heard Phil Gardies' grunt of surprise, saw him pitch forward.

He clawed his way hand over hand along the rope and up the steep bank. He set foot on the road's edge to see Gardies lying two strides away and alongside his thrashing downed animal.

He doubted that Gardies was ever aware of his being there. The man struggled to hands and knees and was trying to scramble beyond the reach of his pony's flailing hooves when the downchopping swing of Evan Rue's .38 caught him squarely on the back of the head.

Limply, already unconscious, Phil Gardies pitched face down against the frozen ground as his animal struggled to its feet and bolted away.

Ben Britt had hitched fresh teams to his stage at the Bear Creek station at sundown, having enjoyed his supper with the Majors family and having delayed his departure as long as he could in hopes of seeing Nancy, Majors' daughter, alone. He didn't manage that but was nonetheless in good spirits as his two teams pulled the battered and empty old Concord into the pass road.

He stopped two miles beyond Bear Creek to light the coach's two lanterns and to refresh himself from the bottle that always rode beside him jammed between cushion and seat brace. He buttoned the collar of his coat and wrapped a weathered strip of canvas about his legs before swinging his whip and cracking its thonged end expertly between his lead animals to send the stage rolling up the road once again.

Britt's lightheartedness lasted until the warmth brought on by the whiskey was gone. He tried to revive it by taking another long pull at the bottle. But the spell cast by Nancy Majors' pretty face and flirting eyes was broken, and presently he sat the swaying seat thinking again of things that had been plaguing him for a long time now. He thought of the stage he had wrecked, he thought of Hester and her constant worrying, he thought of the day in and day out drudgery that netted him a poor living, he thought of Nancy Majors and her affable but too-watchful father. He took another drink and bundled himself tighter against the crisp cold.

Ben Britt often slept on the long climb to the top of the pass, relying on the quickened hoof clatter of his animals to waken him so that he could use brake and reins to negotiate the tricky down grade. Tonight he was slightly dozing when he sensed that signal and with an effort sat straighter and peered into the flickering wan light cast by the lamps.

It was perhaps a minute later when he saw something that made him half rise, lean quickly back against the reins and step hard on the brake. He had to pull his teams sharply aside to keep them from running down a sprawled figure in the road. And finally he walked them partway up the slope before setting the brake, lifting a lantern from its bracket and climbing down.

He saw Phil Gardies lying there, saw the wide hat nearby, and the blood staining the mud-splashed snow. He breathed, "God a'mighty no, Phil," as he knelt and stuck the lantern's stem into the deep snow at the road's edge.

His hand was shaking as he thrust it in under Gardies' coat and felt of the man's chest. And his held breath let go in gusty exhalation, when he felt Gardies' heart beating steadily.

How'd he get here?

About to draw his hand away, he paused, feeling a bulky rectangular object wedged in Gardies' belt beneath his shirt. Immediately curious, he unbuttoned the shirt and drew out a flat telescope leather cigar-case. For a moment he sat back on his heels looking down at it in puzzlement, thinking that he had never seen Phil smoke anything but a cigarette. Then he pulled the case open.

A compressed sheaf of banknotes unfolded and fell to the snow alongside his boots. Britt's mouth fell open in utter amazement. Then he noticed the denominations of the bills and was held spellbound with wonder.

He looked quickly at Phil's face, finding the man's eyes closed and his expression as peaceful as though he had purposely stretched out here to rest. And now a furtive quality was in Britt's glance as he leaned over and started picking up the money.

Wild and unreasoning thoughts raced through his mind. He stopped counting the money when he held a thousand dollars in his hand, calculating the risk he would run in pocketing this much, in dragging Phil down into the trees below the road and driving on.

A thousand dollars. With this much money, no more, he could . . .

He was greedily studying the banknotes when all at once he looked beyond them to see Phil's eyes wide open and staring at him.

Blood rushed to his face. Jamming the money back into the case, he said with false heartiness, "Man, am I glad you've come to. What the devil you doing 'way —"

Phil suddenly moved, his right hand stabbing in under his coat. For an instant Britt sat there too surprised to stir. Then he saw Phil draw the gun.

"Don't," he yelled as the weapon swung around at him.

Phil Gardies' eyes shone with a live fury. Britt knew that the man intended killing him and he struck out frantically, somehow managing to snatch Phil's wrist and keep his hold.

"It wasn't me, Phil," he shouted as he felt the powerful thrust of the arm bringing the gun down in line with him.

He distinctly heard the click of the weapon's sear as the hammer was drawn back. And now he dropped the leather case and brought his other hand up to clamp it on Phil's wrist. He threw his weight forward, hands above his head as he fell across Phil's chest.

They struggled silently then, Phil trying to wriggle from beneath Britt's weight, the stage man spreading his legs wide to keep from rolling over. Phil was the stronger of the two but Britt managed to keep him from bending his arm.

Phil gathered himself for one last convulsive surge of strength. He finally bent his arm and, using his free hand, pushed himself partway from under Britt. But then Britt panicked and suddenly pinned the arm against Phil's chest, one hand turning the gun's muzzle downward.

The Colt's deafening blast seemed to pound Phil Gardies' frame against the ground. Britt felt the man's muscles loosen gradually, then go limp. And Phil's face, a foot from his, grimaced savagely in pain and shock.

Britt pushed away and came to his knees a moment after Phil's expression went slack, after his eyes had closed. His narrow chest heaving, Ben sat there staring down at the blackened hole in the front of Phil's coat, and at the spreading stain ringing the hole.

Chapter 5

For one wildly desperate moment Ben Britt clung to the hope that Phil Gardies might still be alive. He reached out and shook Gardies by the shoulder, shook him hard. The way the man's head rolled loosely against the snow instantly killed his hope.

He stayed as he was, on his knees, staring wide-eyed at the body for a full minute, terror holding him rigid. Finally he could stand it no longer and lunged to his feet, turning away and cupping his grimy hands to his pasty face as he tried to think. He was trembling as though shaken by a bone-deep chill. And suddenly he was feeling a craving for something to steady his nerves.

He hurried across to the stage, climbed to the front wheel hub and reached for the bottle. After two full swallows of the raw liquid he could feel warmth creeping through his thin frame. He took tobacco and papers from his pocket and, dropping the bottle in the pocket of his coat, put his back to the spot where Gardies lay and tried to roll a smoke.

His shaking hand twice spilled the tobacco,

and after the second attempt he crumpled the paper and tossed it aside. He had hoped that the whiskey would calm him, give him courage, but his breathing was still shallow and rapid and he was as afraid as he had ever been.

They don't hang this on me, he thought, trying to rouse himself to a degree of indignation that would give the words some substance. But they fell flat and held no meaning in the face of his stark fear, so that he once again uncorked the bottle and drank.

Slowly now his frantic thoughts did steady to the point where he could reason halfway rationally. Thinking of what he was to do, his first impulse was to take his best animal from harness and ride as far from here as fast as horseflesh could carry him. But then he saw that such an act would point to his guilt as certainly as admitting to the killing publicly.

It next occurred to him to hide Gardies' body and neither by word nor act ever betray any knowledge of what had happened to the man. The notion seemed so foolproof that he eagerly turned toward the body, a surge of relief in him. But then he saw his boot tracks imprinted on the snow, and the patch of crimson marking the spot where Gardies' head had been lying when he first found him. He saw the wheel tracks of the battered Concord marking the fresh snow above the road. And he knew instantly that, if Gardies was missed and someone should look around up here, all this sign would give him away.

Finally, with that deep despair once more settling through him, he knew that he could do only one thing, take Gardies' body on down to Alder. He would have to concoct some foolproof story to give the sheriff and Doc Emery, the coroner.

It was in trying to think what could have logically happened to Gardies that robbery occurred to him as a likely possibility, this bringing him face to face for the second time with the temptation of taking all or part of the money, at least as much as he'd had in his hand not five minutes ago.

He tried to shut out all thought of what a vast difference a thousand dollars would make in his life, at the same time eyeing the banknotes scattered near the body. Their fascination gradually strengthened until he found it impossible to look away. And in the end he stepped quickly over there, scooping them together in a disorderly bundle and stuffing them into a coat pocket without knowing even approximately what amount he was taking.

Excitement had shallowed his breathing. He was finding it hard to believe that Gardies could have been carrying these thousands of dollars. He had the momentary thought that the man might possibly have broken into the bank and rifled Baker's safe. Yet the idea was so ridiculous as to make him laugh nervously aloud.

That sound of his voice came to him as a mockery and directly afterward it struck him sharply that someone might know about this money. If anyone did know that Gardies had been carrying such an amount it naturally followed that the exact amount would also probably be known.

This certainty stirred a new torment in Britt. And he squatted there miserable and unmoving for a considerable interval, his confused thinking turning first one way and then the other, his hunched-over shape elongated in a grotesque shadow by the coach lamp's pale glare.

All you did was find him lyin' here in the road, dead as a man ever gets. You don't know nothing about no money. You didn't search him, so how could you know if any's missing?

Ben Britt listened to that inner voice and tried to believe he could make such a story sound convincing. But he had long ago lost his brash confidence. And now slowly and certainly the feeble spark of his courage died. Finally, angrily, he took the money from his pocket, stuffed it into the case and thrust the case inside Gardies' shirt.

After it was over, as he was dragging the body across to the stage, he was feeling a keen and heady relief. He even began to believe that his story of having found Gardies lying dead here along the road would have a ring of truth to it.

He was feeling better as he lifted the body into the coach and stretched it out on the floor. He went back for his lamp. He saw Gardies' gun lying there, picked it up and thrust it into a pocket of the dead man's coat. He put the lamp in its socket, climbed to the seat and unwound the reins from the seat-brace.

By the time he had swung the teams back down onto the road he was convinced that no one, not even Hester, would ever know exactly what had happened up here along the pass below Rocky Point.

Jim Harbour was awake well before dawn the next morning, as was his habit. He was cooking his breakfast before he suddenly realized that this was Thanksgiving.

Reflecting upon the many things he should and did give thanks for, he was sobered by thinking of what a trial this day would be for Renee and Phil Gardies, more especially for Renee. And over the next three hours as he restlessly worked outside doing the chores and then repairing the burned wall of the lean-to, he was thinking of the girl and of what the future held for her and for Bit.

It was almost eleven o'clock when, as he was measuring a board and getting ready to saw it, a sound from the meadow made him look up to see a buggy pulled by a single animal coming along the ruts his wagon had made yesterday and the day before. He felt a stir of expectation and pleasure in thinking it might be Renee Gardies. But then, knowing how impossible that was, he laid the saw down and walked on out from the lean-to. And in a few more moments he was surprised at seeing that the buggy's lone passenger was George Wickwire.

The rig was rolling to a stop close ahead of him before he caught the seriousness of the gambler's expression. Then, before he could speak, Wickwire unceremoniously announced, "I could use some of your coffee, Jim. It's so far been a poor Thanksgiving. Ever attend a double funeral?"

"Double?" Jim echoed. "Gardies' and who else's?"

"Phil Gardies."

For an instant Jim was merely puzzled. Then a thunderstruck, dumbfounded look came to his lean face. Wickwire saw that and nodded gravely. "It's a fact. Didn't think you could know. Thought you ought to."

"Phil dead?" Jim's voice was hollow, lifeless. "How did he die?"

"He was shot. Ben Britt found him lying up along the pass road last night. If I hadn't had my hands full I'd have come out last night to tell you."

The numbness and bewilderment holding Jim made him blurt out haltingly, "But Renee . . . What's to happen . . ."

His confusion throttled his words. And the saloonman put in gently, "I know. It about floored me, too. It's more than any man should be asked to take all at once, let alone a woman."

"Where is she, George? Have you seen her?"

"I have. Went to the service this morning. Thought maybe there was something I could do, though the good Lord knows what. She was . . . well, call it just plain magnificent."

A look of rising indignation was in Jim's eyes now as Wickwire went on, "Hadn't realized how much of a woman she'd become." He climbed from the buggy and lifted out the tether weight, snapping it to his animal's bit-ring.

The outrage and the fury that had been smoldering in Jim suddenly exploded as he knotted a fist and with a short, hard jab hit the rim of the buggy's wheel alongside him. He swore time and again, his voice hoarse, bitter.

When his words finally trailed off impotently, Wickwire drawled, "You sound like I did last night when I first heard about it. Hurt your hand?"

Jim had been rubbing his bruised knuckles and glanced down at his hand wonderingly, as though only now realizing what he had done. The gambler didn't wait for him to answer but took him by the arm, saying, "Now for that coffee."

They went on into the cabin, Wickwire tossing his hat onto the rumpled bed before taking a chair. He watched Jim with mute concern for all of a minute, watched him lift a lid of the stove and drop in some wood, watched him take down two heavy china cups from a nearby shelf and then move the graniteware coffee pot onto the front of the stove.

Only then did he say, "Ben found him up there to this side of Rocky Point. Shot through the heart by someone who stood close enough to scorch his coat. His horse turned up at Bit sometime after midnight, according to the way the sheriff tells it. By the time a man from town got there with the word, Neal was worried enough to have the crew up and ready to ride."

Jim's glance swung around, a chill look in his eyes. "Anyone tell you why Phil was riding the pass last night?"

"Yes. Tom Murchison."

"Was any of the money gone?"

Wickwire shrugged. "If so it wasn't mentioned. Someone said they'd found a lot on him."

"What about Rue?"

The gambler smiled. "I was wondering when you'd get around to asking that." . . . He slowly moved his head from side to side . . . "There's the puzzler, my friend. Rue was at the church this morning. He was also in town last night, because when we found out where Phil had been going, and why, I insisted that Parks send out and have him brought in. The surprising thing was that Rue admitted he was on the pass road at about the time Phil was. He was on his way to Bend to wind up that cattle deal."

"But it was today he was going across there," Jim bridled.

"So it was. His story is he changed his mind and decided to make the trip last night instead. Because he'd be missing a good Thanksgiving feed if he went across today, was how he put it. He paid his money to Pierce —"

"Someone got the word to him of what Phil was doing."

The gambler lifted his hands in a spare gesture. "How could that be? Anyway, he was back home by midnight. Parks sent a telegram to the town marshal in Bend this morning and got an answer back that Rue was seen on the street and at the hotel around ten o'clock."

"Which would put him on the pass about the time Phil was there?"

Wickwire nodded. "Rue admits all that. But he says he never saw hide nor hair of anyone either coming or going. He would've met Ben's stage somewhere along the road except that he took the old Smuggler mine trail down the far side to save time."

"Like hell," Jim drawled with a cold and wicked anger. "He was hiding in the brush when Ben went past him."

"Now wait, Jim. Ben says he must've passed the Smuggler trail right after seven o'clock. Which, if Rue is telling the truth, means Rue was down the trail well before then. But that early, according to Tom Murchison, was too early for Phil to have got that far."

Jim lifted the stove's lid and stirred the fire with hard jabs of the lifter. "So Rue's sitting sweet and easy."

"That's about how it adds up. One more thing, though. Rue didn't know why he was being brought in. He was wearing his gun. I was there when Parks looked it over. There was dust in the barrel. But Phil's had been fired. One shell. Ben found it lying in the road near him."

Jim sighed helplessly. "Who's gone up there to take a look around?"

"No one yet. Parks said something about doing it late this afternoon. He's invited to the Bakers for a turkey dinner and didn't seem inclined to miss it."

"Doesn't he know it was murder?" Jim burst out. "Doesn't he want to find out who did it?"

"Who knows? Anyway, the coroner's jury has called it 'assault with intent to kill by person or persons unknown.' Parks asked the jury to meet early this morning on account of the girl. Didn't want to drag it out for her any longer than necessary. She agreed it was best to make it a double burial instead of waiting."

The coffee was steaming and now Jim filled both mugs, bringing one across to Wickwire. "You must have an idea on this. What's your guess?"

"I've given up on the guesses." Seeing the way Jim's glance hardened, the gambler went on tersely, "That's the truth. If friend Rue did this he did it with a rabbit's foot in every pocket and with someone besides himself looking after him. Since I'd doubt that God would be on his side, I'm stumped."

He saw no break in Jim's flinty look and continued, "Put yourself in Rue's place. If he pulled that trigger, why wouldn't he have dragged the body off into the brush somewhere to be found next spring when it thaws? And why wouldn't he take the money, go whole hog so long as he'd gone far enough to kill?"

"Then we've got him admitting everything, owning up to being on the road when Phil was. The man's got brains, Jim. If he put that bullet through Phil he'd damn well have come back to Crow Track and kept it quiet about being within twenty miles of the pass at the right time. You know and I know his crew would back him."

Jim's anger cooled enough now to let him see the logic of this reasoning. His thinking was confused and had reached a dead end. Dismissing any further conjecture about Rue, he mentioned the thing that had been uppermost in his mind since first hearing the news the gambler had brought. "What'll happen to Bit now? To Renee?"

"You know as well as I what's bound to

happen. Unless . . ."

When Wickwire hesitated, Jim asked, "Unless what?"

"Unless something happens you haven't told me about." A quality of wryness was in the glance the gambler gave Jim then. "You're like me, keep your affairs pretty much to yourself."

Puzzled, Jim said, "Don't follow you."

"Tom Murchison tells me that three nights ago Raoul Gardies asked you to work for him."

"Oh, that."

Jim picked up his cup and crossed the room to sit on his bed as Wickwire soberly observed, "Can't blame you for turning him down. Not then."

"But you'd like to see me change my mind now?"

The chip-on-shoulder quality of Jim's tone made the other answer mildly, "You're your own man. You know what's best."

"Suppose I should go over there? What can one man do to stop what's coming? There's no law on the books that says Rue and his tribe can't move in from the north and east. It's open —"

Wickwire waved a hand almost tiredly in a gesture that made Jim pause. "Sure, you've got plenty of reasons for not giving a hoot about Bit. So let's talk about the weather. Think it'll be snowing by evening?"

Jim couldn't hold back a smile, though in a few more seconds he was serious once more. "All right, I decided ten minutes ago I was going to Bit. But tell me what I can do to help that girl? What can I?"

The other shrugged, though his look was a pleased one. "Didn't bring my crystal ball along, Jim. But something'll turn up."

Turning to look out the cabin's back window beyond the foot of the bed, Jim drawled, "Speaking of snow, suppose it does snow before Bill Parks has stuffed his gut and gets up there on the pass to have his look?"

"I was thinking of that."

Gulping the last of his coffee, Jim came erect. And George Wickwire, following his friend's example, came across to set his cup on a counter alongside the stove, asking, "Mind if I tag along while you look it over?"

The long drive home in the surrey with Tom and Carrie Murchison exhausted Renee far more than the ordeal of the burial service. She was discovering that the years had made a garrulous old bore of Tom Murchison, for he talked incessantly throughout the two hour drive to Bit. To keep from listening, Renee thought of anything but of what he was saying. She tried to put herself in Paris, imagine herself talking to friends back there. She found herself carrying on long conversations in French with people she hadn't thought of for weeks, and this mercifully helped her endure the drive.

When the surrey pulled in below the house, Renee suddenly knew she couldn't face eating her Thanksgiving dinner with these two. Carrie gave her the opportunity she was looking for as Tom was helping her down from the rig. "Now, honey, you go in and lie down while I help Madge get the turkey on. You'll feel better after a little rest."

"No, Carrie. I don't want to rest and I couldn't swallow a mouthful of food." Renee turned to Murchison. "Tom, would it be asking too much for you to go tell Neal to saddle the sorrel and bring him up here? I'd like to get away for an hour or two."

"Go for a ride on a day like this?" Murchison was amazed and glanced up at the cloud-darkened sky. "Why, the sun isn't even out. It's raw and cold, liable to snow, and —"

"It's what I'd like to do, Tom. Would you mind?"

"Well, if you say," he reluctantly agreed. "Want me to come along?"

Renee shook her head, turned and left

them, going up to the big empty house and to her room. She tolerated as best she could Carrie being with her as she changed her clothes. And when she finally rode the sorrel away half an hour later she was feeling a keen relief.

Instead of following the road south, she struck off across the trackless range to the north, thinking that by doing this she would avoid meeting anyone. The morning-long tension seemed to have knotted her insides, even her brain. She had doggedly held her emotions in check all these hours except for one brief moment at the end of the service. And now as she dropped across a gentle rise to put Bit headquarters out of sight behind her it seemed that her lonesomeness and heartsickness could no longer be endured, and she let the tears come.

There was no trace of self-pity in her as she gave way to her grief. And presently when it had spent itself she felt better, the tension gone, nothing but longing and sadness left in her.

It was getting colder now, the clouds were darker, and as a sharp gust made her draw the collar of her coat tighter she was finding the awesomeness of the responsibility that had been thrust upon her almost frightening. Across the rolling, whitened sweep of land ahead she could see small bunches of cattle on the move, just a few of hundreds all across Bit's broad range that were this afternoon drifting toward the shelter of low ground.

She had learned enough of working cattle to realize that raising them was a man's art. Furthermore, managing a ranch the size of Bit called for the know-how of perhaps one man in a thousand. And when she thought of the responsibility for all this resting with her there was an alien uncertainty in her.

Her outgiving nature rebelled at the thought of how few men there were to turn to for help now. Lew Neal was a stolid, unimaginative man who had leaned heavily on her father for advice. Baker in at the bank could probably take over the books her father had kept all these years. There were only those two, no others.

But then there's Jim Harbour.

The thought struck her suddenly and stirred in her a feeling of warmth, almost of tenderness. But then when she remembered his polite refusal of yesterday a momentary hope that had thinned her depression slowly died away.

Yet she found it oddly pleasant to think of this man who had so stubbornly defied her father, of the clean, strong lines of his face, of the sure way he handled himself and of the unfeminine delight she had experienced yesterday in watching him so soundly thrash Nye.

She found herself wishing Lew Neal could be half the man Harbour was. And now she was remembering how annoyed Phil had been with Neal yesterday, annoyed because in trying to be helpful the man had been constantly with them, not seeming to realize that she and Phil might want to be alone. Phil had been so brusque with him just as he was leaving for town that it had been almost as though he had wanted to tell her something he preferred Neal not to hear.

She was stirred from her preoccupation now as, topping a long and gentle slope, she came within sight of the Salt Flats camp lying in a shallow saucer-like depression half a mile ahead. Its disorderly clutter of pens and sheds, its rickety wooden windmill and the sagging pole fences were all quite familiar to Renee. She could look back and remember years ago spending a week here with Phil during calving time, could recall the chilly before-dawn breakfasts, the long hours in the saddle and how she had bottle-fed several weak and sickly calves.

It surprised her to notice smoke fanning out from the chimney of the work shack, and out of curiosity she put the sorrel across there.

She was perhaps a hundred yards short of the shack when its door opened and a man with a rifle slacked in the bend of an arm stepped into sight.

Apprehension gathered in her as she went on toward him, at length reining in ten yards from where he stood. *He hasn't been around the place,* she told herself, observing that he was middling tall and gaunt, cold of eye and badly in need of a shave.

She tried to ignore his plainly unfriendly stare, tried to smile as she said, "I was just riding past and thought I'd look the place over. We'll have to do some work on it before next spring."

"You the Gardies girl?"

His blunt question was spoken in a belittling tone. And Renee answered tersely, "I am."

"Then put this down in your book," he stated flatly. "My handle's Dooley. This is my place. I filed on it yesterday. So any fixin' up that's to be done will be my lookout, not yours."

Renee could feel her face get hot as she realized that this must be one of Rue's homesteaders. She was instantly furious. "Why, my father built this —"

Dooley suddenly let the rifle fall from its elbow hold, caught it by its grip, rocked it level. Its unexpected blast marked the exact instant a puff of snow jumped into the air barely a foot from the sorrel's left hoof.

The animal shied, tossing its head, and it was all Renee could manage to keep him from breaking as Dooley told her, "Get this. You Gardieses are through, hear? Now clear out."

That this man was dangerous was obvious. It was also obvious that he had no more respect for her than he would have had for a man. And a real fear blended with her outrage to make her rein the sorrel quickly around.

As she started away, Dooley called, "Tell your mangy crew to keep clear of me unless someone wants to argue my bein' here. If they do, they'd better come packin' iron."

Renee was trembling with indignation as she left the Salt Flats camp behind. She doubted from the way Dooley had spoken that he knew of Phil's death. *You Gardieses are through,* he had said, and the indictment kept repeating itself in her thoughts, filling her with a sense of futility and impotence stronger than any she had so far experienced.

She was still feeling badly shaken at the end of the long ride home. She was much relieved at finding the Murchisons gone, at no one but Madge, the cook, being in the house. When the woman concernedly tried to persuade her to eat something, she answered, "Later maybe. Right now I'm cold, Madge, cold to the bone. What I need is a hot bath."

Madge brought her two buckets of steaming water from the kitchen range's reservoir, and as she presently lay back in the tub and felt the warmth going through her some of the inner chill left by her encounter with Dooley slowly melted away. She had thought of lying down and resting but found when she finished her bath that she was too restless to think of sleep.

She dressed and went on into the big living room. The first thing that met her eye was the horsehair sofa where her father had died in his sleep just twenty-four hours ago. She forced herself to stare at it over a deliberate interval. And it pleased her to discover that she was little stirred by this sight she had suspected might unsettle her.

When she turned away she found the room's feeble light depressing and began lighting the lamps. She was trimming one of the wicks on the double lamp at the big room's center table several minutes later when she was startled at hearing a knock on the porch door.

She was annoyed at thinking that this could be no one but Tom or Carrie, or perhaps both of them. But when she went to the door and pulled it open it was to find Jim Harbour, hat in hand, standing there.

She was surprised and pleased. "Come in, Jim."

He stepped in and closed the door gently, his look very grave. And without preliminary he told her, "George Wickwire came up to tell me about Phil." Over a brief and awkward pause, he added humbly, "There ought to be something a man could say at a time like this, Renee." . . . He lifted his hands outward, let them fall to his sides . . . "There just isn't."

"I know. But it was good of you to come anyway."

His eyes thanked her for having helped him over this uncomfortable moment, for letting him know that she didn't blame him for the thought that had sent Phil on his ride. Then he was saying, "I'm here to stay if you still want me."

Renee experienced a quick lift of delight and gratefulness. Yet at the same time some obtuse and proud facet of her nature rejected the terms on which she was getting Harbour's allegiance, and before she had quite willed it she heard herself asking, "You're doing this because you're sorry for me?"

"Partly," he admitted. "But there are other reasons."

"Could you tell me what they are?"

He frowned in thought, trying to find a way of expressing a thing he had never expected he would be putting into words. At length he told her, "After what happened last night I can see what you were trying to tell me the other day. What your father tried to tell me. There's been a murder. Which means Rue and his pack are dead wrong regardless of their rights. Yesterday I didn't think he'd dare go as far as he did with Murchison. Now today he's gone the limit. I won't see myself lined against Bit in company with that tribe."

"Suppose they hadn't gone as far as murder?"

His wide shoulders lifted, fell. "I'd have come anyway. Last night I began to see it. Raoul Gardies wasn't taking anything from anybody in settling here. The troubles he had were always because of someone trying to take something from him. Rue's trying it now and Rue is wrong."

He was plainly roused, openly angry. She saw that and said gently, "This is what I've been wanting to hear you say, wanting you to believe." The smile she gave him was fleeting, overshadowed by a look of concern. "But what's to happen now? Can you tell me?"

"No. Haven't thought it out yet."

"Do we let Rue bring his cattle in?"

"That's up to you. I'd say to let him come

so far, no further."

"You mean we'll keep him off that range between Crow Track and the Springs?"

He nodded. "We ought to try."

"But you've said yourself that he and these others have a right to do what they're doing. Do we break the law to stop them?"

"Rue was the first to break the law," Jim bridled. "If he gets out of line so much as an inch you should shove him back."

Suddenly she was smiling again, this time with a real merriment in her eyes. "Jim, you begin to sound a lot like my father."

"I should sound a lot like him," he said, knowing that she had been baiting him. Then, struck by a thought, he went on, "There may be one thing you can do to out-smart the man and keep him where he belongs."

At her puzzled look, he told her, "Yesterday George Wickwire sold me some federal warrants that let me buy a section of land around my place. Just in case Rue got the notion to move in. Wickwire has more of these warrants. With them you could buy all that east country Rue's after. George might even have enough to let you take up the land around those north homesteads so no one can move further onto your grass."

Renee's glance showed a hesitant eagerness. "Is it that easy?"

"It is if you have the money, around a thousand dollars a section."

"But I hardly know George Wickwire."

"Let me see him about it. Might even go in tonight." His glance all at once betrayed an uneasiness she didn't understand until he asked gently, "Renee, do you mind my asking something about last night, about Phil?"

"Not at all. Why?"

"Who knew Phil was taking that ride? Who besides you?"

Renee's brows arched in surprise. "Why, Baker in at the bank knew it. And Neal. Then when Tom and Carrie got back from town I told them." She eyed him in puzzlement. "You're thinking Rue might have known?"

He nodded soberly. And when he didn't speak she shook her head. "Tom was at the inquest. Much as he hates Rue, he had to admit that he thought the man was telling the truth."

Jim was on the point of coming out with something but then abruptly decided against it. An hour ago he and Wickwire had found the place on the pass road below Rocky Point where Phil Gardies had died last night. Though it had already started snowing, though most of the maze of sign was sifted over and had meant little to Jim, it had been impossible to miss seeing where Rue had waded the snow as far as the stump to tie his rope. And, across the road, Jim had seen the man's deep tracks leading down and in behind the aspen. More than that, he had found what looked like a rope burn on the tree's trunk where the bark had been shredded down to the bare wood.

Though he suspected that someone had stretched a rope across the road to throw Phil's horse last night, he now realized that he could easily be wrong. Such guesswork gave him no right at all for causing Renee to hope that the riddle of her brother's death was any nearer a solution.

She had been eyeing him quizzically and now said, "If what you're thinking is true, Jim, it would mean that either Tom or Neal rode across to see Rue last night. I know it wasn't Tom because I was with him and Carrie most of the evening. As for Neal, dad trusted —"

"Let's just forget it, Renee. It was only a wrong hunch."

He hoped he had made his words convincing, though he had already decided to ask some questions of the crew about Neal's whereabouts last night. And in another moment he knew that Renee was satisfied as she asked, "Rue isn't going to like it if we can buy that land, is he?"

"Not much."

"The others won't either." She was remembering what had happened to her a little over an hour ago and added, "Perhaps I should have told you before this, but I rode up to the Salt Flats this afternoon." And she went on to tell him about Dooley.

When she had finished, Jim's bleak look of suppressed rage made her wonder if she had been right in letting him know what had happened.

And when he drawled with deceptive mildness, "Might be interesting to find out how he'd stack up against a man instead of a woman," she wondered even more.

The light was fading over the Salt Flats draw when Dooley came out of the shack carrying an empty bucket and headed for the windmill. He had taken half a dozen strides beyond the shack's blind southeast corner when suddenly the slam of a sharp explosion jerked the bucket's bail from his grasp.

As the bucket clanged to the frozen ground, Dooley spun sharply around, crouching, and his right hand blurring to the holster thonged low at his thigh. But when he heard the slap of a rifle's breech closing and glimpsed the tall shape standing near the shack's corner, when he saw the rifle held lazily at arm's length but pointed squarely at him, he instantly froze, moving not a muscle and his bony fingers wrapped around the handle of the Navy Colt's.

Jim Harbour eased out from the wall and sauntered toward him, the Winchester held slack. Dooley, the tension beginning to go out of him, went rigid as the rifle exploded without warning a second time. A chip of ice blasted from the ground very close to his right boot sharply stung the back of his hand and he cried out softly, involuntarily.

Harbour's step hadn't broken, and now he levered a new shell into the rifle's chamber and came in behind Dooley, who felt the weight of his gun all at once leave holster. The next moment the rifle's muzzle prodded him sharply against his spine and he was told, "In you go."

Stark fear knotted Dooley's stomach muscles as he started for the door's rectangle outlined by lamplight from inside the shack. He experienced a moment of wild hope in thinking of his rifle hanging inside above the door. But as he entered the shack his courage failed him at hearing the crunch of Harbour's boots close behind him.

The door crashed shut with a force that rattled the shack's one west-facing window.

Dooley had crossed the small room to stand alongside its sagging bed, and now he turned slowly about to find Harbour leaning against the door lazily inspecting the shack's disorder and dirtiness.

Abruptly Harbour was hefting the Winchester, drawling, "The Gardies girl tells me you're mighty handy with one of these things." He reached to a pocket now, took out two shells and thumbed them through the rifle's loading-gate, adding, "By the way, I hired on to work for her this afternoon."

Dooley's dark face showed a sickly yellow pallor now. He managed somehow to say in a croaking, trembling voice, "I figured . . . it looked like she'd come here to . . . to warn me off, Harbour. How was I to —"

He lunged violently aside and sprawled onto the bed as the rifle all at once lifted in line with him. The weapon's deafening explosion left his ears ringing. Immediately afterward the flue of the stove behind him hit the floor with a hollow bang.

A fog of soot was settling over Dooley and his bed then as Jim Harbour levered in another shell. "I was told to pack along some iron if I came across here."

"Listen, I . . ."

Dooley's feeble words broke off as he saw the rifle's hammer drawn back once more.

Harbour was holding the gun at arm's length as he swung it a fraction of an inch. This time its thunderclap explosion was prolonged by the clang of the dutch-oven bursting apart, by the splash of Dooley's supper stew spilling to the floor.

Held by a paralysis of panic, of outright terror, Dooley watched then as Harbour lifted the rifle to hip level and levered five more quick shots that filled the shack with a prolonged thunder. Dooley saw his wall-hung saddle swing violently as two bullets ripped through its tree. The dishpan was whisked from the table and clattered to the boards. A bullet smashed the window's single pane. And finally Dooley cringed back, then was jolted hard as a front leg of the bed broke under the heavy smash of lead.

An awesome silence settled over the room then. A wicked, cold smile patterned Harbour's lean face as he reached back and rested the Winchester against the wall.

Dooley hadn't noticed his Colt's at Harbour's belt until now as the man reached for it, drew it with left hand. Then Harbour was saying, "They tell me you could cut a lot of notches in this thing if you wanted, Dooley. Here, catch it."

In the split-second Harbour's arm drew back, then tossed his gun at him, Dooley noticed two things. First, Harbour's right hand hung ready to reach to the holster along his thigh. Next, he saw that Harbour was still smiling.

He had instinctively reached out to catch his weapon. But instantly now he jerked his hand back. The Navy Colt's hit the wall behind him, thudded to the floor.

Jim Harbour let his hands hang loosely at his sides. "Pick it up. Make your try."

Dooley had seen this man fight Shep Nye yesterday. He had been impressed by what he saw. Now that he was faced with making a choice, he found himself impressed by what he had seen this last half minute.

The bright, killing light in Jim Harbour's eyes was what decided him. He simply sat there, not moving, his glance falling away.

Jim said flatly, "I'll stop by now and then to see how you're getting on, Dooley." He reached for the rifle, pulled open the door and stepped outside.

He walked the two hundred yards to the north and over a rise to where he had tied his gelding to an outcrop of granite well out of sight of the shack some twenty minutes ago. Sliding the Winchester into its scabbard, he pulled on the coat he had left tied to the saddle, climbed astride the black and headed into the southwest.

In fifty more minutes the winking lights of Alder lay close ahead. As he came into the foot of Main Street he noticed the Britt house and, on sudden impulse, turned in toward it. He opened the yard gate and went up the path to the porch wondering what, if anything, he could learn from Ben Britt that George Wickwire hadn't already told him.

Hester Britt answered his knock on the door. Worry was plain on her face even before he asked her if Ben was at home, before she answered, "No. The sheriff came for him almost half an hour ago. I don't know where they went."

He rode up the street idly wondering what reason Bill Parks could have for wanting to see Britt this evening. On his way past the courthouse he noticed lamplight shining through the drawn blind on the street-facing window of the sheriff's office and dismissed the idea of going in there. He could find Britt later, after he had seen George Wickwire about the land warrants.

Evan Rue waited until it was full dark before riding the last mile to Alder. Instead of following the road into the foot of Main Street, he angled across and took the alley to the west, riding it as far as the rear of the courthouse where he dismounted and tied his bay behind the coal-shed.

This had been a day-long wait for him and he hurried as he crossed the alley, then tried the back door of the courthouse. He breathed a sigh of relief when he found the door unlocked, as he had told Bill Parks this morning it should be.

He walked the stale-smelling corridor to its street end and was pleased at seeing a slit of light showing under the door to the sheriff's office. He entered the room without knocking, at once glancing quickly at the single window as he closed the door, noting relievedly that the blind was drawn.

Bill Parks had swung around from his desk at the sound of the door opening. He raised his brows and was about to speak when Rue told him, "Go get Britt."

The law man frowned. "Now, Ev, let's think this over. We got —"

"Bill, Ben Britt's a confounded liar and you and I know it. You're to get him and bring him here. Right now."

Parks knew the Crow Track man well enough to tell that it was futile to argue. He said mildly, "Me, I'd let sleepin' dogs lie," as he came up out of the chair, crossed the room and reached his hat down from a rack on the wall. On his way out of the door he muttered, "Hope you know what you're doing."

During the quarter-hour the sheriff was gone, Rue paced the office impatiently, the dull anger that had been in him since last night slowly mounting to a higher pitch. He was worried, had been ever since late this morning when, cutting through the timber above Rocky Point, he had discovered Harbour and Wickwire looking over the spot where he had last night left Gardies lying on the road.

There was an uncomfortable interval for him when he finally heard someone coming in from the street, for he couldn't be sure who it was and he had no wish to be seen here. But when the office door abtuptly swung open on Parks and Britt his uneasiness left him.

He saw at once that the stage man's face wore a wary look of concern, and with only this much to go on he fixed Britt with a scowling stare and snapped, "Sit down."

Ben looked from Rue to the sheriff, then back again. "Wish someone would tell me what —"

"Sit down."

Britt knew Evan Rue's ugly temper. It cowed him now and his look was worried as he took a chair in the corner facing Parks' desk.

Rue ignored his one-armed friend as he came over to stand glowering down at Britt, catching the whiskey taint of the man's breath.

"Ben, you'll either own up to the truth about last night or I'll tie you to that chair and club you. Now what did happen up there?"

Britt tried to appear indignant but managed only to look frightened. "I've told Bill every —"

Rue suddenly lashed out and struck him a hard open-handed blow across the mouth. "Talk, damn you."

The stage man ran a hand across his lips, glanced down at it to see it streaked with crimson. And now his eyes showed a sullen alarm. "Sheriff, it ain't going to listen so good for you when I tell it around how I was treated."

Parks was obviously not liking this, yet a brief glance from Rue warned him not to speak. Then in another moment the Crow Track man was drawling, "Suppose I tell you something I haven't let on about so far, Bill. You've heard how I was up on the pass last night?"

Britt nodded reluctantly. He was suspicious, on his guard as Rue blandly continued, "What I haven't told is that I heard your shot. 'Way off in the distance. It got me to wondering, so I came back. I was coming around the point above when I spotted the lights of your rig below. Directly after, I saw you go on. You were half a mile ahead so I said the hell with it and turned back."

Ben Britt's face was losing its color as he protested, "But I tell you I just found him layin' there already dead."

"Then what did your shot mean?" Rue was leaning over him now, glaring down at him. "What did it?"

Britt gulped. Parks was watching him and all at once realized that Rue had stumbled onto something. He came over alongside Rue, saying, "Ben, this is already enough reason to lock you up. Tell the rest."

Suddenly Britt straightened, no longer afraid. "You said you rode down Smuggler last night. How could you hear my shot from all that —"

He clamped his jaw shut as he realized he had said too much. And the next moment Rue breathed, "So you did shoot him after all."

Terror laid its hold on Britt. He had been living a nightmare since last night. The unbearable weight of it now put a panicked look in his eyes as he blurted out, "He was to blame. He thought I was swiping his money and here all I was doing was picking it up. He pulled his gun. He killed himself, I tell you. The thing went off while I was trying to grab it out of his hand."

Rue turned away, nodding to Parks. "Lock him up, Bill."

"But you got to believe me." Ben's voice

rose hoarsely. "He did it, not me."

"Sure, Ben," Rue told him. As an afterthought he said, "There's nothing to worry about. Bill will get Doc Emery to call a new jury. You just tell them what you've told us and they'll let you off. Like you say, it was an accident."

A miserable hope lighted Ben Britt's eyes now as he looked at the sheriff. "Is he right, Bill? Will they turn me loose?"

Parks nodded slowly. "From the sound of it, Ben." His one hand reached to pocket and brought out a ring of keys. He went to the jail door and unlocked the big padlock, saying as he swung the door open, "We'll get a fire going in here and you'll be right comfortable."

Ben Britt stood up, looking at Rue in such a beseeching way that Rue told him, "No hard feelin's, Ben. But they're trying to pin this on me, so what else could I do? Now we're both in the clear."

The stage man nodded meekly and followed Parks into the jail. Over the next several minutes as he listened to the sounds and voices issuing from the jail, Rue stood in thought. He took a twist of tobacco from his pocket, bit off its end and tongued the chew into his cheek. By the time Bill Parks came into the room once more and swung the door shut, Rue knew what he was going to do.

The law man, on his way to the chair behind his desk, said, "Ev, that was a good hunch, a fine piece of work."

He had eased his ample bulk into the chair before Rue spoke. "He admitted everything, eh, Bill? How he met Gardies up there, how Gardies told him where he was going and what for. How Gardies showed him the money."

Parks looked up in surprise. "What the devil you talking about?"

"He's about broke, has been for months," came Rue's enigmatic words. He thought of something then that sharpened his glance, made him ask, "Where's the money you found on Gardies?"

"Locked up right here." The sheriff wagged his thumb in the direction of a small safe along the wall beyond his desk "Why?"

"How much money is there?"

"Baker said this afternoon there's five thousand. What with everything I've had on my mind today I haven't got around to counting it."

"Let's count it now."

"See here, Ev. What you driving at?"

"Get the money."

Rue's look warned Parks of something and he got up out of the chair and went to the safe, saying in irritation, "Let you get a thing in your head and you're like a mule."

He opened the safe, took out Phil Gardies' telescope leather case and tossed it to the desk. Rue had pulled the case apart, taken out the money and was counting it even before the law man came to stand at his elbow.

"Five thousand it is." Rue thumbed through the banknotes again, abruptly dividing the bundle and handing Parks most of it as he laid the smaller portion on the desk. "You can put that back," he said.

The law man warily eyed the money on the desk. "What's that for?"

"That's the thousand that was missing tonight when you got around to making the count. That's what Ben took out of his boot when you finally got the truth out of him just now after you'd threatened to beat his brains out."

Bill Parks' eyes opened wide in alarm. "Now look here," he burst out. "I'll know more about this before it goes any further."

Rue smiled thinly. "You balkin', Bill?"

The sheriff's face reddened. Before he could say anything, Rue went on, "Let's keep things going along nice and smooth like they are. You were hell on wheels at Shiloh and with Andrews on his raid up from Marietta. Weren't you, Bill?"

Parks' one fist clenched. Then, suddenly

deflated, he asked dully, wearily, "What is it you want me to do?"

"Ben admits he was crazy drunk or he'd have known he couldn't get away with it," came Rue's matter-of-fact answer. "He'd climbed down off his rig and was talking to Gardies, seeing all that money. He lost his head. He caught Gardies when he wasn't looking, grabbed his gun and shot him. Then he took a thousand dollars, no more. He loaded Gardies into his wagon, brought him down here and told how he'd found him laying dead up there along the road."

The law man had reached across his sagging paunch with his one good hand and rubbed the stump of his other arm. "It's good as far as it goes. But Ben can call me a liar."

"Ben won't ever call anybody anything ever again, Bill."

The full impact of what Rue had been leading up to hit Bill Parks now. And as his look took on awe, Rue nodded down to the law man's Colt's worn in a holster high at the hip.

Parks breathed barely audibly, "No, by God. Not me."

The Crow Track man smiled sparely once more. "Didn't think you could work up the guts." He reached out and lifted his friend's gun from leather. "The way you tell it is that you were standing in there leaning against the bars talking to Ben, everything free and easy between you. Then he reached through, grabbed this quick as a rattler and did it."

The law man let his breath go sharply. "Why not let things ride like they are now?" he begged. "He's admitted what happened. Let it stay that way."

Rue shook his head. "No, Bill, I caught Harbour looking around up there on the pass today. You think I'm a mule? You've never run across one till you know Harbour."

"But what's up there for Harbour to find against you?"

"That's what I don't know. That's why I want this settled once and for all." Rue's probing glance studied his friend's face a moment. "Got everything straight on how you tell it?"

"Lord, Ev, you're not thinkin' straight. There's got to be some other way."

"There isn't."

Parks shook his head tiredly. "When do we do it?"

"Now." Rue held out a hand, his left, since he was holding the law man's gun in his right. "Let's have the key. Then you can go out and have a look at the street. We don't want anyone around."

The sheriff reluctantly handed his keys across, then hurried out into the hallway, plainly wanting no part of this. His damp forehead felt chill as he stepped outside. He breathed deeply as he looked both ways along the darkened street. The windows of the *Niagara* and the hotel's glassed veranda were the only ones showing lights tonight.

He could see a man leaning against the railing of the hotel steps. He heard someone going away along the plank walk opposite. Aside from these two, the street was deserted as far as he could tell.

Finally, reluctantly, he went on back and into his office. The jail door was standing wide and he heard Rue saying, "Just don't fret, Ben. Bill can cook up something to keep Hester from worrying."

Britt's voice came then. "She don't deserve a thing like this. We got to leave here, get away and make a new start."

Parks heard the scraping of bootsoles. Then suddenly Rue was standing in the jail doorway, a questioning look on his narrow face. The law man nodded, saying quietly, "All clear."

Rue gave him a look of disgust, of contempt, before turning back through the door. Parks noticed that his cedar-handled gun had replaced the horn-handled .38 in the Crow Track man's holster. Then he was hearing Rue ask, "Everything all right, Ben? Warm enough? Got plenty of tobacco?"

"Guess so. But I could sure use a drink."

"I'll have Bill bring you a —"

A deafening explosion pounded across Rue's words. Parks clearly heard Ben Britt's catch of breath, heard a soft thud. Then Rue was lunging out of the jail and across to the hall door, snatching his Smith and Wesson from the desk as he passed it.

On his way out of the office, Rue said sharply, "You haven't laid eyes on me since this morning in church, Bill."

Chapter 6

Two minutes ago Jim Harbour and Wickwire had decided to go down to the courthouse to see what Parks had wanted of Ben Britt. They were crossing the intersection below the saloon, their boots squealing against the frozen mud and snow, when the muffled pound of a gunshot rolled up out of the downstreet darkness.

Jim slowed his stride and the gambler looked around to ask, "Now who'd pick that way to celebrate the Thanksgiving?"

A man who had been leaning against the railing at the foot of the hotel steps straightened and faced the lower street. When he suddenly turned and hurried away, Jim said sharply, "Must be trouble," and quickened his pace.

They were well beyond the hotel when they saw the man ahead joined by another, the two halting in the light shining from the window of the sheriff's office. And in another moment Jim recognized Bill Parks as the second man.

He and Wickwire came in on the pair to hear Parks saying, ". . . happened so fast I couldn't stir. He'd been blubberin', I was trying to quiet him down. All of a sudden he reached through the bars, grabbed my forty-four and put it to his chest."

Seeing Jim and Wickwire, the law man added brusquely, "One of us ought to run and get Doc Emery."

"That'll be me."

As the man who had come from the hotel hurried away into the shadows, Parks muttered, "There isn't a prayer he's still alive." His breathing was shallow and fast, his jowled face was pale and there was a genuine solemnity to his tone as he added, "He knew where to point that gun."

"You haven't said yet who it was."

The sheriff glanced up at Jim. "Ben Britt. Shot himself right here in my jail."

Having halfway expected this answer, Jim was still shocked by it and asked, "Why would Britt want to kill himself?"

A pair of men coming from across the street briefly took Parks' attention. "Why? Because I'd just finished slapping the truth out of him about last night. Because he never found Gardies lying dead in the road. Because he killed Gardies himself."

"He admitted that?" Wickwire asked incredulously.

"He did." . . . The law man raised his voice

now for the benefit of the two men approaching . . . "I'd slipped up on something. Counting the money we found on Gardies. Today Baker told me he'd left town with five thousand dollars. Tonight I got around to counting what we took off him. A thousand was missing. So I brought Ben up here, sat him down and went to work on him. After he broke down he took the thousand out of his boots."

"But Britt was no killer." Jim's tone was disbelieving.

"Don't take it out on me," Parks bridled. "I'd of said he wasn't either. But he admitted to being hog drunk. He was nearly that just now. Claimed he didn't know what he'd done last night till after he'd fired the shot."

He avoided Jim's hard stare and Jim said flatly, "Gardies wouldn't have been careless enough to let a drunk kill him with his own gun."

"That's what stumped me," the one-armed man insisted. "Ben said he'd never've stopped to talk to Gardies if Gardies hadn't called out to him. Seems Gardies' horse had gone lame and he wanted to look the hoof over by the light of Ben's lamps. Ben got down to help and he told him where he was going and why. Even told him about the money."

When he hesitated, Jim drawled, "Go on. What's the rest of it?"

Parks' further embroidery of the details came without hesitation. "Ben said he'd been broke so long he went plain crazy hearing about so much money right there by him. All he had to do was step in and grab the gun when Gardies was bent over prying this stone out of his nag's hoof."

He was eyeing Jim again and what he saw on Jim's face made him add testily, "I'm telling you what Ben told me. Don't you believe it?"

Jim's glance swung briefly to Wickwire. He was thinking of what he had found up along the pass road today, and now he ignored the gambler's warning shake of the head, saying, "Not a damned word, Sheriff."

Parks' jaw thrust out belligerently. His one good arm waved toward his office window. "Hell, he's in there dead, killed by his own hand," he almost shouted. "I didn't shoot him, didn't have any reason to. The money he took out of his boots is in on the desk. Go see for yourself."

"I'm going to."

Three more men had joined the group and now followed Jim, Wickwire and the sheriff up the courthouse steps. On their way through the door, Parks muttered, "You keep this up, Harbour, and I'll drag you into court."

Jim checked a caustic answer, knowing how

pointless it was to argue when he lacked any facts but that meager sign he had found on the pass road to back his suspicion that Parks either wasn't telling the truth or had unknowingly been made the victim of some quirk of circumstances.

"There's the money," the law man said as they came into the office, pointing to the banknotes on his desk. "And here's Ben."

He led the way into the jail. After a brief look at the body and the gun lying beside it, Jim moved out through the gathering crowd and into the office again. Parks followed and now growled, "You satisfied?"

The sheriff turned away abruptly as he saw Doc Emery coming into the room. He pushed in through the jail door, calling, "Let the doctor through."

Wickwire stepped over alongside his friend. "Easy, Jim. We could be wrong about this."

"We could be right, too," was Jim's stubborn answer.

Doc Emery spent a scant quarter-minute in the jail. When he reappeared, the hum of talk filling the office quieted at once. "Ben was probably dead before he hit the floor," the medico said. His glance went to the sheriff. "Has anyone been sent to tell Hester, Bill?"

"No one yet." Parks looked around. "Anyone like to take on the chore? Because I damn' well won't."

No one answered and an awkward silence lay over the room until George Wickwire quietly said, "I'll go."

"Fine, George. Be as easy on her as you can."

"That should be a simple matter," the gambler drawled in thinly veiled sarcasm.

He turned then and followed Jim into the hallway, and they were on the way down the steps outside when he observed, "Worse things could have happened for Hester."

"Suppose so." Jim was still baffled and angry as he came to a halt on the walk now. "How does this strike you, George?"

Wickwire shrugged. "You can't argue against facts."

"There's one I'll argue. Britt was too weak in the knees to kill himself, drunk or sober."

"Wouldn't be too sure, Jim. I knew a thing or two about Ben. He was a mean, wicked devil with drink in him. Why, I've known him to . . ."

When he paused, as though having been on the point of saying something he might regret later, Jim drawled, "You're forgetting what we found up on the pass this morning."

The saloonman frowned. "What you're trying to say is that someone else shot him?"

"I'm only saying there's something damned queer here. Rue managing to get to Bend last night instead of today to buy that herd. Phil killed on his way there. Britt telling one story last night and this morning at the inquest, then another tonight to Parks. And without any witness present except our hero himself."

He heard the door behind him opening and turned to see Doc Emery coming down the steps buttoning his overcoat, black bag in hand.

"What a Thanksgiving for Hester, poor girl," the medico said as he joined them.

"Doctor, did you see anything out of the way in there?" Jim queried. "Anything at all?"

Emery's grizzled brows lifted. "Nothing except that Ben did a better job of it than I'd have guessed he had the nerve to."

He thought of something then that made him chuckle softly. "Funny how a man's imagination sometimes runs away with him. When Simpson came to get me, when he told me what had happened, I took it for granted we had a murder on our hands. Because of something I was sure I'd heard maybe five minutes before Simpson knocked at the door. But then as I was leaving I asked Agnes about it and she told me I was mistaken."

"Mistaken about what?" Jim wanted to know.

"Agnes and I had been in the kitchen doing the supper dishes and I thought I heard someone riding out the alley. But Agnes was positive I was wrong. I'll take her word for it because her hearing's a lot better than mine."

Jim gave the man a frowning glance. "Couldn't she be the one who's wrong, doctor?"

"Hardly. I'm getting a little deaf as age creeps on. Also a little absent minded. What I thought I heard tonight was something I probably heard last week, or even a month ago and just now remembered." Emery shrugged and, turning away said, "Good night, gentlemen."

They watched him disappear down the walk and Wickwire said, "He's right. He is getting a little feeble."

"But he still could've heard something, George."

"Doubt it. Even if he did it needn't mean anything." The gambler took his watch from pocket now, glancing at it and thinking of his self-imposed errand. "Eight-twenty. Well, I'd better get this over with. Like to come along?"

"Rather not, George. But . . ."

"But what?"

"If you get the chance, ask Hester about Ben. How he acted. What he said. Tell her

. . . Would it be wrong to tell her we think Ben didn't shoot himself?"

"It would be till we have better reason for thinking he didn't. Let me see how things go." On the point of turning away, Wickwire asked, "Where'll you be?"

"Waiting right here."

The saloonman nodded and walked away. He was ill at ease, wishing one moment he hadn't spoken back there in the office, glad the next that he had. He knew the path to the end of the street so well that he could have walked it blindfolded, could have told exactly the moment he would reach the stretch of brick walk fronting Judge Bullock's house and finally the low, muddy spot to this side of the Britts' picket fence.

He turned in the gate before the house thinking, *Now she'll be leaving for good,* the thought disheartening and making him feel all at once dead inside. He removed his hat as he knocked on the door's frosted glass panel, and when he heard her steps sounding across the room inside he was dreading what the next few minutes were to bring, wanting to be far away from here.

Hester Britt's look was a blend of surprise and pleasure when she saw who it was. The lamplight striking her face showed him that she was red-eyed, that she had been crying.

And without preliminary he gently asked, "You already know, Hester?"

She nodded, stepping back from the door. "Yes. Agnes Emery thought I should. She's just left." Her hesitant glance was studying him as he came in and pushed the door shut. "I . . . she didn't know for sure. He's dead, isn't he?"

Wickwire nodded mutely and she turned away, lifting her hands to her face. He wanted very much to step across and take her in his arms. Yet he stood as he was, embarrassed, glancing quickly around the room. He was at once struck by its color, by a fleeting impression of its lightness and warmth exactly suiting this girl's personality. Then she suddenly turned to face him once more with a bright-eyed look of defiance.

"I won't believe it," she breathed. "He was so frightened when the sheriff came. Last night and today he'd been cross. I suppose he was drinking. But before he left with Parks he kissed me and whispered something very strange. Then he was gone before I could ask him about it."

"Just what was it he said, Hester?"

"Something I couldn't understand, still can't. Something about their not being able to do anything to him for what he'd done. Then he told me, 'We were fighting over the gun. Because he thought I was after the money.' Now I wish I'd gone with him. Or I should have told someone. Like Jim Harbour or you. Harbour was here right after the sheriff took him away."

Wickwire was thinking, *Then Jim could be right,* as he told her, "Don't blame yourself for this."

"But Ben simply wouldn't shoot himself." Her eyes were brimming with tears once more.

He felt helpless, an intruder. Then it was as though she realized how awkward she was making it for him, for she tried to smile. "I'm sorry to be carrying on this way. I suppose I'm just being a hysterical female."

"You're not." He checked the impulse to tell her that she wasn't the only one who had found something strange in Ben's death, instead asking, "Will you be wanting anything? Help of any kind in closing up the house and leaving?"

She shook her head. "Thanks to you I needn't worry." Then, very firmly, she told him, "I'm staying, George. Selling the business to you, or to someone else if you don't want it. But I won't leave. It would be . . . be too much like running away from something. As though I was ashamed of what Ben had been."

George Wickwire had rarely experienced the thankfulness and the sheer delight her words brought him. He had never before quite faced the bald fact of his loving this girl. Yet now he did face it with a humility and a finality. And the realization put an unintended double meaning to what he told her now. "If you stay I buy only half the yard, Ben's half. And since I'd be so much dead weight, you'd draw a salary. Unless . . ."

When he paused, she asked, "Unless what, George?"

"Unless you'd object to having a tinhorn as a partner," was his half-joking, half-serious answer.

A quality of strong awareness was in Hester's eyes then, as though she was for the first time catching the subtlest understanding of her being something other than just another person to this man. The realization brought color to her face, put a softness in her glance as she said, "You're simply George Wickwire. You should be proud of what you are, not ashamed."

"Sounds like you mean that."

"I do mean it."

He was somehow feeling a better man then as he asked, "It's agreed?"

"It is if that's the way you want it."

Once again a feeling of awkwardness was

in him. He didn't want to spoil this moment by lingering, by any further talk. So he simply turned to the door.

Hester must have understood his mood and been in sympathy with it. For as he stopped in the doorway she only smiled faintly and nodded her goodnight, saying nothing.

He went out across the yard and turned onto the street with thoughts that were hard to define, that were very grave yet remotely tinged with a near-happiness. He didn't deceive himself by pretending that he was sorry Ben Britt was gone. He simply wished that Hester would be spared what she was going through. Along with the wish came the certainty that the future would hold more for her than the past had. And suddenly he knew that these past minutes had changed his life, that his day-to-day existence had ended and that he had something beyond his own simple wants to look forward to.

Some of this feeling of quiet purposefulness betrayed itself as he walked in on the courthouse steps to find Jim Harbour waiting in the shadows. "Your hunch may be proving out," he announced, and went on to tell Ben Britt's last words to his wife.

He noticed the cold, alert look that came to Jim's face, saw the way his friend's glance went to the nearby window of Parks' office, and cautioned, "This bears a little thinking out, Jim."

"Why does it?" Near-forgotten instincts were coming alive in Jim now, telling him that the time for patience had ended. "They've hauled Ben away and things have quieted down in there. Parks thinks he's pulled this off, whatever it is he's not telling. So we go in, tell him what we know and watch him try and crawfish out of it."

"Crawfish out of what, though?"

"Who's to know till we throw it up to him?" Jim regarded the saloonman in a puzzled, half-angry way. "You just said yourself he's not telling all he knows."

"But wait a day or two till we've had the chance to —"

"Wait, hell." . . . Jim was suddenly struck by the change these past three days had worked on him, by how inevitably certain discarded principles out of his past had caught up with him . . . "The time for waiting's done with, George. You and I should have gone straight to Crow Track today. To look over some ropes, beginning with Rue's. I shouldn't have put off coming here to see what Parks was up to with Britt. Maybe I shouldn't even have turned down old Gardies' offer in the beginning."

Wickwire was awed by this unlooked-for

outburst. "But you've had good reasons for doing what you did."

"Maybe they weren't so good. There's been a lot of dying that —"

"That you couldn't have done anything about even if you had gone to work for Gardies."

Jim turned impatiently up the steps toward the courthouse door. "Want to be in on this?"

"Not much. But more than I did a minute ago," came the saloonman's sober reply.

On their way into the hall they met a man who had just come out of the sheriff's office. "Bill's closing up for the night," he told them. When neither of them said anything, he shrugged and went on out.

They found Bill Parks alone in the office, swinging shut the door of his safe. At the sound of their steps he looked around, took the key out of the safe door and came erect. "I could stand some sleep," he said wearily. "This has been one sweet mess."

He frowned as Jim pushed the door shut. "Look, I'm ready to go. Can't this wait till morning, whatever it is?"

Jim said, "No, Sheriff." He came on across the room, shoved the desk chair out of his way and stepped in on the law man. Before Parks knew what was happening Jim had reached out and lifted his gun from holster.

Then, as he stiffened in surprise, Jim took him by his good arm, spun him around and pushed him down into the swivel chair with such force that it rolled back and into the wall.

"Now we'll have it," Jim drawled, looking down at him. "What really happened in here tonight, Sheriff?"

Bill Parks' look became indignant. He swore. He started up out of the chair.

Jim reached out and pushed him back down again, saying very quietly, "We've been down to see Hester Britt."

"Should that mean something?" Doubt and wariness thinned the law man's belligerence, though he tried to look incensed.

"Ben and Gardies were fighting over the gun, she says. Gardies the same as killed himself."

Parks breathed an angry, impotent sigh. "Every damned thing I know about this is what I got out of Ben. I've told it all. Wish now I'd called in somebody as a witness."

"Wasn't there a witness, Sheriff?"

"You know there wasn't."

"Then who rode out the alley right after the shot?"

Wickwire could almost feel the impact of those words on the law man. Until this moment he had been halfway sorry for Parks, pitying him for having to undergo Jim

Harbour's cold and remorseless questioning. Yet suddenly now the man's sureness was gone.

Jim saw it, too. He eased back half a step and leaned against the edge of the desk, saying, "George, go back and see if the alley door's open." Then, as Wickwire's boot tread sounded along the hallway, he took tobacco from pocket and carefully built a smoke, his glance not straying to his hands but regarding Bill Parks with a steady, cool watchfulness.

The gambler was gone for perhaps ten seconds, and during this interval the law man sat glowering at the floor, trying to maintain his offended attitude. Then abruptly Wickwire came back into the room, announcing, "The door's open."

"If it's open, old Reed forgot to lock it after he swept out last night." Parks sat straighter in the chair, glaring up at Jim now. "This is enough of this fool —"

"Who was it, Sheriff?" It was Wickwire who spoke, his tone larded with contempt. "Who was in here with you to work Ben over? Who left right after the shot? Was it Rue?"

The law man shook his head almost savagely, as though having reached the end of patience. "The last I saw of Rue was in church this morning. Now the two of you can damn' well back off or I'll have warrants out for you."

"There's just one more thing, Parks," Jim said quietly. "George and I were up on the pass today looking around. We found where a rope had been stretched across the road to trip Phil Gardies' horse. It wasn't Ben Britt that stretched it, either. Now do you talk or do we go at it another way?"

The one-armed man's manner abruptly underwent a change. First he frowned, as though thinking through what Jim had told him. Then, quite seriously, he asked, "You aren't stringin' me along?"

Jim made no reply, his hard glance studying the man so intently for several seconds that Parks' look wavered and finally dropped away.

Wickwire read his meaning into that and shortly intoned, "Bill, you look like the cat that swallowed the mouse. You know for a fact we aren't stringing you along. You know it was Rue who stretched that rope. You know Rue killed Gardies. And, by all that's holy, you either killed Britt tonight or helped Rue kill him so he couldn't talk."

A desperate look was in Bill Parks' eyes now. For an instant it appeared that he was about to lunge up out of the chair and bolt for the door. Then his loose face slowly sagged into a lifeless expression and he muttered dully, "I stick by what I said. You can talk all night and I'll not say different."

Jim glanced briefly around at the gambler and the look that passed between them made him shrug, come erect and step around the desk to pull open the jail door. Eyeing Parks, he tilted his head toward the cells. "In you go, Sheriff."

The law man gripped an arm of the chair with his hand, a panicked look in his eyes. "What're you aimin' to do?"

"Hold you in your own lockup till I can get out and bring Rue in."

"Damned if you do."

Wickwire came in on Parks now, saying ever so gently, "Bill, get in there before I shine a boot on the seat of your pants."

Renee had told Jim that she would be waiting up for him regardless of how late he returned to Bit, and after she had eaten a late supper she went to her father's room and began sorting through his things, packing most of them in two big brass-bound trunks. She had expected to find this chore distasteful and wanted to get it over with quickly, yet as hours passed and she finally had most everything arranged she realized that this had been quite a pleasant evening despite the nostalgia and feeling of melancholy it had roused in her.

She was surprised shortly after ten o'clock at hearing Lew Neal and Madge talking at the far end of the hallway, then presently by Madge appearing at the bedroom door to announce, "Lew's here and says he has to see you. Says it's important."

"Send him in, Madge."

When Neal came into the room, Renee saw at once that he was uneasy. He stood awkwardly waiting until he heard Madge's door closing. Then he bluntly said, "Murchison tells me Harbour's here."

"He isn't at the moment. But he's come to work for us."

"Does that mean I'm out of a job?"

Renee disliked the man's truculent manner and now, sitting on her father's bed, she told him, "Not unless you want it to mean that."

The unexpected firmness and aloofness of her tone robbed Neal of some of his unaccountable grouchiness and he stated warily, "A man's got to know where he stands."

"You stand exactly where you did this morning. Or yesterday or the day before." Neal irritated her, especially now as she remembered his insensitiveness of yesterday when she and Phil had wanted so to have a few minutes to themselves. "Do you object to Harbour being here?"

"Reckon he's no better than me for what we're up against."

"Just what are we up against, Neal?"

"Why . . . why, these jokers bringing in them cattle."

He had obviously been thrown off balance by her question, and now some perverse streak in her nature made her ask another. "If you were me, what would you do about them?" When he responded with nothing beyond a puzzled stare, she insisted, "What would you? Have you thought of anything, done anything?"

"I just do what I'm told," he stated doggedly.

"Then that's why Harbour's here. Because I can't tell anybody what to do about all this. Because he seems to know a little of what should be done."

Suspicion crept into his glance. "Like what, miss?"

"Like Phil trying to get to Bend to buy those cattle." She was on the point of telling him about Jim's idea of buying the land warrants from Wickwire, then caught herself as she remembered what Jim had said earlier. And quite suddenly it seemed not such an impossible thing that someone could have warned Rue of Phil's ride to Bend, so that before she quite realized where her thoughts might lead her she was asking, "By the way, Neal. Did you tell any of the men where Phil was going last night?"

"No. Why would I?"

"Because Harbour's fairly certain that Rue somehow knew what Phil was doing."

"How could he?"

Renee was shocked at what she saw on Lew Neal's face. His pretended anger failed utterly in masking the guilt and the alarm in his eyes as he asked testily, "You mean he thinks I took the word to Rue?"

"Did I say that?"

"The same as." He avoided her glance now, nervously rolling and unrolling the wide brim of his hat.

She let the silence draw out for several seconds after his sullen answer. She was awed by the implications of what she had just seen on the man's face, hardly daring to trust an intuition that told her Lew Neal had betrayed her.

Presently, in a voice that trembled with emotion, she said, "If Harbour's right, if someone did warn Rue, then that man killed Phil as surely as though he fired the bullet."

He stiffened, suddenly eyeing her with a raw challenge. "Damned if I'll take this. From you or anyone else."

He turned sharply and was halfway out the door when she came up off the bed saying sharply, "Neal."

Stopping, swinging around, he glared at her defiantly. "I've not accused you or anyone else directly," she told him. "But if someone did this thing, that man had better kill a horse getting as far away from here as he can. Because it'll be either the horse or him, if I know Jim Harbour."

"Before God, miss, it wasn't —"

"You can go now, Neal."

The Bit foreman started to speak, checked himself. Then abruptly he swung around and was gone.

The closing of the outside door along the back hallway was a sound that stirred a momentary panic in Renee as she realized what she had done. She could be very wrong. Her emotions had been strained nearly to the breaking point for better than a day now, and as she thought back over their conversation she felt less sure of herself, almost convinced that Neal's look of guilt had been entirely of her own imagining.

As the minutes dragged on, she was nearly beside herself. She longed to go to bed, to let sleep rid her of her doubts and the sense of having wronged Lew Neal. Yet she had promised Jim that she would wait up for him, for word of how George Wickwire had reacted to the question of the land warrants.

For a time she debated going down to find Neal and apologize. But in the end she knew she would only be laying herself open to ridicule, perhaps to abuse. For nothing she could say would make amends for what her words to him had implied. She was positive she had lost the ranch a foreman, was sure that he would be here in the morning to draw his wages.

Finally a restlessness and a longing to have Jim Harbour here to steady her drove her to her room to get the heavy cape and then go outside. The stinging cold of the night air was bracing and seemed to help slow the confused run of her thoughts. She decided to walk and wear down the nervous tension binding her brain so tightly, and she went down the steps and started out along the lane, not wanting to miss Jim if it should happen that he got back while she was out of the house.

She had been walking for perhaps five minutes when she caught the sound of a trotting horse shuttling in out of the distance. Her pulse quickened at the thought that this could be no one but Jim. But then the next moment her depression returned as she thought, *Suppose it isn't?*

As the sound of the oncoming animal

strengthened she began walking faster in her eagerness. Then finally, when the rider came in out of the darkness, she was running. She recognized Jim's tall shape and cried out in thankfulness and relief, calling to him.

He had been half dozing in the saddle, wearied of his troubled thoughts. And her, "Jim, is that you?" jolted him with such hard surprise that he instantly reined the mare to a stand.

Seeing her shape close ahead, he swung quickly aground, alarmed by the high-pitched quality of her voice. The next moment he was sure that something was wrong as she ran to him, took a tight hold on his arms and buried her face against his chest.

She was out of breath and he could feel her trembling as she cried softly, "How I've wanted you, Jim. I've done a terrible thing. To Neal. You've got to help me make it right with him."

He tilted her chin up so that he could look down into the pale oval of her face. "Nothing's that wrong, Renee. Tell it from the beginning."

He could feel the giving in her, the unconscious way she sought the assurance of his physical presence then as he put an arm about her waist and she began talking. And presently she was saying, "I just wasn't thinking straight. Because of what you said about Rue knowing."

"You were thinking straighter than you could've guessed."

The pressure of this girl's willowy and slender body against his arm brought a sense of her nearness he found suddenly unsettling. Because of his sharp physical awareness of her, and because he realized what an instinctive trust she was placing in him, he stepped away from her now and reached over for the mare's reins, feeling that to prolong this somehow intimate moment would be to give it a meaning it shouldn't have.

He reached out then and took her arm, turning her toward the house as he said, "Ben Britt was killed tonight, Renee. In the jail. George Wickwire and I don't like the look of it." And he went on to tell her of all that had happened in Alder.

"But I don't understand, Jim. What could Britt dying possibly have to do with Neal?"

"Maybe nothing. Then again maybe a lot. We locked Parks up on the same brand of hunch that made you think Neal knows more than he's telling. Doc Emery may or may not have heard someone going out the alley after Ben was shot. The back door of the courthouse may or may not have been left unbolted by accident. But what Ben told Hester can't be argued. He was scared when he said it, it's got to be the truth."

They were coming in on the wall below the yard now and as Jim shortly led the mare to the rail to tie her, Renee asked, "If what Ben told Hester was true, doesn't it mean that Rue couldn't have killed Phil? Even if he used the rope as you say he did?"

Jim nodded. "That's about it."

"Then why did you say just now that you have to go across to Crow Track tonight to see if you can find the rope that skinned that tree?"

"Britt's dead, Renee. George and I don't think he killed himself. And there doesn't seem to be any reason why Parks would have done away with him. But if Rue stopped Phil up there along the road last night, if he stopped him the way I think he did, he'd have the best reason for wanting Britt out of the way. Especially if it could be made to look like Britt had confessed to an out and out killing."

"But will finding his rope prove anything against Rue?"

"It'd be a start toward proving something. Catch a man off his guard, throw a scare into him and things usually happen." Jim glanced toward the path leading to the working buildings of the ranch. "Want to go see Neal now and get things squared away with him?"

"I don't want to, Jim. But it's got to be done."

They started down the path walking side by side. And shortly Renee was saying, "You must pick some good men to take across there with you tonight. Tom would love a chance to —"

"No, Renee. This is a one man chore. One man going in late."

She stopped short, and as he faced her she breathed, "You're going alone? How can you think of it?"

"Because I don't want to stir up any trouble, get anyone else tied up in this. A man setting about it the right way can go in there and come out again without anyone even knowing he's been around."

"But suppose something happens?"

He smiled sparingly. "Now you sound like Wickwire. He wanted to side me."

"He should've wanted to." Her tone was very grave. "Jim, I won't let you do this."

For the second time that night he took her arm, leading her on as he told her, "All right, have it your way. Neal can go with me."

"Neal and three or four others."

"Just Neal. The others would only be in the way."

They kept on arguing, Renee stubbornly, Jim quietly trying to convince her that he ran little risk considering the lateness of the hour and the fact that Rue's crew would be asleep. Finally, reluctantly, she was persuaded.

Lew Neal lived in a room over the harness shop, and as they were approaching it Renee noticed lamplight shining from the upstairs window and murmured, "I'm so ashamed, Jim. We'll have to make it up to him in some way."

"Just tell him you were upset, that you never once meant he could have done it."

She shook her head, sighing worriedly, and as they climbed the outside stairway to the upper landing she reached back to take his hand, clenching it tightly and whispering, "You'll have to do most of the talking."

The door was ajar, standing open six or eight inches. Jim's knock on the panel pushed it further open. They stood very close to each other over the brief interval they waited for an answer. And when it didn't come, Jim called, "Lew, you there?"

As the seconds ran on with no sound coming from the room, Jim finally shrugged and, reaching out, pushed the door wide.

Renee caught her breath at what she saw. The room was a shambles. The bed was torn apart, its mattress half-lying on the floor. A deal bureau was slanted out from the wall, its drawers lying nearby, empty. Scraps of paper were strewn about the boards, a rotten, ripped tarpaulin lay in one corner.

Jim looked around at Renee, soberly drawling, "You were right after all."

Lew Neal was gone from Bit.

Neither Harry Talbot nor Shep Nye had any liking for the chore Rue had given them upon his return from Alder. It was cold, getting colder by the hour, and a restless knife-sharp wind that had sprung up around eleven o'clock added to their discomfort by bringing an occasional light spitting of snow out of the north.

In the three hours he had been watching here along the town road, Shep Nye had several times dozed off and had each time wakened to feel the chill penetrating almost to the marrow of his bones. Finally, unable to tolerate it any longer, he broke off his vigil, climbed to the saddle and angled north past one winking light of Crow Track to where Harry Talbot had stationed himself better than a mile away at the timber's edge to watch the north approach along the bench.

"This is a waste of time," he growled as he drew in alongside Talbot. He pulled off his mittens, blew on his hands. "The boss is spooked over nothin'. Harbour's up there at his layout all snug asleep while we freeze on the off chance of his showin' up here. Wonder what the boss found out in town that got him so edgy?"

"No telling. But have a listen at this. Dooley came drifting in a little over an hour ago, around midnight. Packin' all his possibles. Seems Harbour paid him a visit at the Flats along about dark. Shot the insides out of the place. Dooley's scared so bad he's here to collect his wages tomorrow and pull out for good."

Nye whistled, though the effort was spoiled by his still-swollen and bruised lips. "I'm damned." His anger came alive then. "Dooley leavin' when he knows we're after a reason to get the law on Harbour? Don't he know this is what we been after?"

"But it isn't, Shep. Because this afternoon Dooley put his tongue to the Gardies girl. She'd happened by to look the place over. Worse than that, he was fool enough to try and scare her with a rifle, with lead. Guess he figures to clear out before Bit rides him out on a rail."

Nye swore in surprise, and Talbot added, "So the boss may be thinking along the right lines after all."

His slow thoughts having come alive, Nye

asked, "Why would Harbour be caring what happened to a Gardies?"

"Search me. But he cares enough so's he told Dooley he'd hired on to work for Bit."

This time Nye's surprise was so complete that it held him speechless. And Talbot went on, "He must've tied the job he did on Dooley with a nice neat ribbon. Because Dooley just out and claimed he'd never seen the likes of the way the man handles a gun. A rifle, too. All hip shootin', Dooley says. With never a miss."

"Dooley's the man to know." Nye was thinking of something else now and shortly spoke with a weighty concern. "Harry, there's a thing or two's got me stumped. What's going on? The boss showin' up to-night acting skittery as a cat on a griddle. Then take last night. He's being awful quiet about what happened up there on the pass. You think he —"

"Me, I don't get paid to think," Talbot cut in.

"Different here," Nye said sullenly. He thought of something else to complain about. "We stay out here freezin' till along about two, he says. Why so long?"

"Because there are only three of us, with Fred away to help Pierce chouse that herd across from Bend. Mose'll have all he can do to ride circle by himself between two and daylight."

Nye sighed heavily. "Well, guess I better be gettin' back."

He glumly turned the gelding and started away, not riding a straight line as he had in coming here but swinging a wide circle that would take him close behind the ranch buildings. He had some vague notion of perhaps stopping in at the kitchen for coffee, though by the time he came within sight of the feeble lamp glow shining from the back window of the crew cabin he had lost his nerve, after last night not caring to dwell upon what might happen if Rue was still up and should catch him taking his ease.

So he kept on until he was within vague sight of the layout, then swung away so as to avoid being seen. Though the sky was clouded over, the waning moon had nonetheless thinned the darkness these last two hours so that now he could clearly distinguish objects patterned against the grey background of the snow to a distance of possibly eighty or ninety yards.

He was wistfully eyeing the cabin's light, his gelding at a walk, when another pale sliver of light off to his left took his attention.

For a moment he thought he had only imagined seeing it, for now as he looked squarely in that direction it was gone. But a second later he was seeing it again, a flickering beam showing between two warped boards in the wall of the shack by the corral.

His first thought was that it was a fire, or that someone had left a lighted lantern in the shack that also served as a shelter for storing grain and saddles. He had lifted his boots outward, about to spur across there and investigate. But then his naturally suspicious nature made him hesitate. Frowning as the light thinned and died once more, he slowly stepped down out of the saddle and, ground-haltering his animal, started walking toward the shack.

He was perhaps thirty yards from the building's squat outline when he saw the light suddenly flare again. He stopped, tried a long moment to think of something to explain what he was seeing, couldn't. When he went on, trying to walk quietly and to let his weight down gently against the snow crust, he pulled his coat aside and drew his Colt's from belt.

Shep Nye was feeling a little foolish as he covered the remaining distance to the near wall of the shack, convinced as he was that what he had to deal with was most probably a lantern running dry with a glowing wick. Yet he eased in on the wall as soundlessly as he could, breathing shallowly and leaning over to look between the two boards where the light had shown.

Sudden surprise turned him poker-stiff. He was seeing a man kneeling inside the shack and holding a match in one hand while uncoiling a rope with the other. The intruder's back was turned toward him, yet he knew instantly that this was Jim Harbour.

Three other ropes lay on the dirt floor near Harbour. Nye tried to puzzle out the meaning of the ropes for a scant second, forgot them then as a hard elation rose in him and he began weighing what to do next.

Instinct told him he ran considerable risk in trying to rush Harbour, in going straight in there. Then shortly he knew how he would take the man, and, moving slowly, carefully, stepped to his left and to the corner of the shack that put him in sight of its open door. He crouched there, the Colt's held ready.

He waited out a full minute. Nothing happened. Once he heard the scrape of Harbour's boots, another time he caught the sound of the man sighing gently. Then suddenly Harbour's tall shape moved into sight beyond the door.

Nye gloried in seeing that Harbour held a coiled rope in his right hand and that his back was turned. The Crow Track man drawled throatily, "Move and you're dead," rising and drawing back the hammer of his .45.

Jim Harbour went motionless, stunned by the impact of that unexpected voice sounding across the night's utter stillness. He knew it was Shep Nye behind him, knew also that the man would kill him if he tried lunging back into the shack.

"On your face, and reach," came Nye's gloating words then.

Jim let go his hold on the rope he had taken from Rue's saddle two minutes ago. Holding hands outward from his sides, he went to his knees as he heard the crunch of Nye's boots coming in on him. He stretched out full length in the snow, hands at shoulder level. Then all at once Nye's knees slammed down onto his back, driving his breath out in a groan. The hard jab of a Colt's barrel poked the back of his head and he felt his coat being jerked aside as Nye fumbled for his .44.

With a brutal shift of his weight, Nye came erect. "On your feet and start walking."

Pushing himself up and brushing the snow from the front of his coat, Jim looked around to see the Crow Track man standing spraddlelegged and well out of reach.

"Why the rope?" Nye wanted to know. When Jim gave no answer, he drawled, "That can come later. Head for the light."

Jim started toward the bunkhouse light, the

aftermath of his surprise at first hearing Nye's voice loosening all his muscles now, though he couldn't rid himself of the certainty that the man meant to kill him. He bleakly looked back over the last carefully planned quarter-hour that had brought him in here without so much as a moment's hesitation or doubt. He had tied the mare three hundred yards south of the corral in the timber. He had come in up-wind, hadn't alarmed the dogs. Even the four horses in the corral had paid him no attention at all as he circled it to the shack.

The hair rope he had taken from the worn saddle with the ER burned along the skirt, bore a long grey-green stain near its end. He had even been able to pick some curling pieces of shredded bark from its braided windings. It was a thousand to one chance that this was the rope that had been used up on the pass road last night.

They were some twenty yards from the cabin and its light when Nye suddenly bawled, "Mose. Mose, get out here," afterward saying in a lower voice, "Far enough, Harbour."

Jim had barely stopped when he saw the cabin's door swing open before a bright light. Two men stood there, Mose Ehlert holding a lamp and the second man behind him peering into the darkness over his shoulder.

Ehlert called in annoyance, "You're forty

minutes early. Me and Dooley're right in the middle of a game of cribbage."

Nye prodded Jim sharply in the small of the back with the Colt's, pushing him forward, calling, "But look who I got here."

Suddenly Ehlert mouthed an explosive oath, turning quickly to his companion. "See who it is, Dooley?"

Jim's momentary surprise at finding Dooley here at Crow Track was forgotten now as the man pushed Ehlert roughly aside and came out of the door. Watching him, Jim was gripped by a colder wariness that brought all his senses more sharply alert.

On this walk up here he had decided to do what he could to take the punishment he knew Nye would give him in hopes of eventually coming face to face with Rue. But Dooley being here made him wonder if he would ever get to see Rue, and now he slowed his stride, saying, "Take me to Rue, Shep."

"The hell I do. Me and Dooley'll have a little visit with you first. Real friendly like." The gun prodded Jim's spine again. "Go on. Get in there."

Jim now had no illusions whatsoever on what the next few minutes were to bring. Shep Nye would have no pity for him. Dooley had nothing at stake here beyond the salving of his injured pride. And as Jim saw his chances dwindling, all but gone, the streak of fatalism that had once been such a strong part of his makeup was coming to life after these three years when it had been all but forgotten.

He could look back across those years and strip away the change they had worked in him. The old and carefree recklessness, the scorning of odds that had once been part and parcel of his wearing a law badge, stirred in him now. He had a moment's uneasiness, a feeling akin to regret and longing as he thought of Renee and of how he had failed her. But then he put her from mind as he started toward the door, toward Dooley.

Mose Ehlert stepped back into the cabin now, yet the light of the lamp was strong enough to let Jim see the pattern of hate etched on Dooley's unshaven face. The man from the Salt Flats was standing waiting there alongside the door. And now as Jim came abreast him his hand slashed up along thigh, lifting gun from holster.

Dooley whipped the Colt's to shoulder level and swung it at Jim's head in a viciously fast gesture. Jim saw the blow coming, hunched down and stabbed a hand out. He caught Dooley's bony wrist and spun around, throwing all the weight of his big frame into forcing the man's arm back and down.

For an instant Dooley's body was between him and Nye. And as he wrenched the arm backward, as Dooley grunted in pain, he reached out with his other hand trying to get a hold on the gun.

But Dooley's hand clawed open that instant and the weapon fell to the frozen ground. Nye gave a hoarse shout and lunged in at them as Jim felt Dooley's arm suddenly snap.

The man's agonized scream rang in Jim's ears a split-second before the blinding, aching blow of Nye's down-arcing Colt's caught him at the back of the head. He felt himself falling, his numbed senses left him.

Chapter 7

Evan Rue came hard awake out of a restless sleep, the imagined echo of Dooley's shrill scream jerking him bolt upright in bed. Knowing instantly that something was very wrong, he reached to the holster hanging at the head of his bed, threw back the blankets and lunged for the window.

He lifted the sash as high as it would go, leaned out and looked toward the crew cabin. A light showed down there. He saw two figures moving in front of the door. Checking the impulse to call out, he turned and snatched his pants and shirt from the chair by the bed.

A scant quarter-minute later he hurried on into the cabin's main room. He was groping his way in the blackness toward the door when he collided with a table, overturning it, hearing a lamp smash against the floor. He grunted his disgust as he finally came outside and started running toward the light.

He could make out Nye's hulking form now and clearly saw the man kick at a shape lying at his feet. The feeling of alarm built up in Rue to such a pitch then that he bawled,

"What the devil's wrong?"

Nye wheeled at his shout, and Mose Ehlert, who had been kneeling near the bunkhouse door, slowly rose. Rue came in on them to see two figures sprawled in the dirty snow, the one near Ehlert writhing and gripping shoulder with hand, the other lying motionless.

Rue saw that the injured man was Dooley, and just now Nye identified the other by bluntly announcing, "Caught Harbour snoopin' around in the shed by the corral, boss. When I got him here Dooley tried to belt him with his iron. But Harbour grabbed his arm and busted it, looks like. Happened so quick I couldn't do nothing about it."

Dooley lay moaning softly and Rue, giving the man a brief and cursory glance, ignored him and stepped over to look down at Harbour, asking, "Is he dead?"

"Haven't looked."

"What did you do before you booted him just now?"

"Tried to bust in the back of his skull."

Rue knelt and thrust a hand inside Jim's coat, feeling of his chest. "Get him inside," he said as he stood up once again.

Shep Nye reached down, got a hold on Jim's boots and dragged him across and through the door. When Jim's head dropped from the doorsill to the floor with an audible bump, Rue said acidly, "I want him kept alive."

Ehlert was helping Dooley to his feet, and when Rue saw them about to follow Nye he said quickly, "Better take him on up to the house, Mose. He'll just be in the way here."

He held no sympathy whatsoever for Dooley, knowing the man well enough to suppose that he probably deserved what had happened to him. He followed Nye on in now and was annoyed at seeing the Chinaman emerging from his small room in the direction of the kitchen. "George, get on out there and help Mose," he told the cook. And as the Chinaman headed for the door, he went over to Nye, helped him lift Jim onto a bed. "Now let's have it. Harbour was where when you ran into him?"

Nye had barely begun explaining when Rue interrupted him with, "Ropes? Why would he be looking over ropes?"

"Don't ask me. But when he come out of there he had yours. Was taking it with him."

Rue frowned, puzzled, knowing this should mean something. When he failed to see what it did mean he asked tersely, "What's the rest?"

"That's about it. That and what I already told you. If Dooley hadn't horned in we'd of had the chance to —"

"I know. You'd have had someone hold him so you could do what you couldn't yesterday when he could use his hands," was Rue's sour comment. He leaned down now to shake Jim by the shoulder. When this had no effect, he straightened. "Better get some water and bring him to."

Nye, on the point of turning away, asked, "What could he be wantin' with your rope?"

Suddenly Rue thought he knew, and the knowledge was so unsettling that he growled, "Come on. Move."

He watched sullenness settle over Nye's scarred face, watched him go across to take the drinking bucket from a bench by the door and then step outside. Nye left the door open and Rue went across and closed it, feeling the room's chill and stepping over to the stove to drop some wood into it.

The suspicion that Jim Harbour had discovered how he had used his rope last night was sobering, worrisome. He came over to the bed now and looked down at the man, a deep rancor stirring in him. Jim was breathing loudly, almost snoring, and seeing the bloody stain on the grey mattress under the unconscious man's head made Rue wonder whether or not he was going to be seeing another dead man tonight.

Nye shortly came in with the filled bucket.

Rue reached out as Nye hefted it, obviously ready to dump it onto Harbour's head. "Hold on. We don't want to drown him. Get a rag."

They began working on Harbour, first bathing his face, then lifting his head and trying to force him to swallow some of the water. His paleness, his labored breathing and the continued bleeding of his slashed scalp took on an ominous meaning as the minutes dragged by without his responding in any way.

Finally, when a quarter of an hour had passed, Rue said wearily, "Looks like we just wait it out." He turned to Nye. "Better ride on out and bring Talbot in."

Once Nye had gone, Rue brought a chair alongside the bunk where Harbour lay and sat down. Some time later he was stirred from a light doze at the sound of the door opening. Turning, he saw Mose Ehlert coming into the room. Ehlert caught the sober set of his face and came across to look down at the unconscious man.

"Not so good, eh?"

Rue shook his head and Ehlert went on. "It's not so good with Dooley, either. His shoulder's not busted, but it's sure out of joint. He's about off his head. Think I ought to take him in to the sawbones?"

"Might be best," Rue said, hardly caring about Dooley. Then, struck by a thought, he added, "If you do go in, ask around and see if Parks has run across anything more on Gardies."

Ten minutes after Ehlert had gone, Rue heard the cook come into his room from the kitchen end of the cabin. The sounds of George stirring around had barely died away when Nye and Talbot arrived.

Rue got up as they came in. "You two take turns watching him. I'm going up to bed."

Nye walked over and looked down at Harbour. "A good belt across the face might bring him to."

"We'll never know because you're not going to try it." Rue fixed his crewman with a beetling stare. "I mean that." He turned to the door.

On his way across to the house, Rue got to wondering whether or not he had made a mistake in getting rid of Ben Britt. But then, because he invariably believed he was right in all things, he thrust aside his small doubt and hurried on so as to get in out of the cold.

Harry Talbot had just taken a sleepy look at his watch, finding the time to be twenty minutes past four o'clock, when he heard Harbour stir on the bunk alongside his chair. He looked quickly that way, lunged up and away from the bed as he saw that Harbour's eyes were open and that the man's long frame had tensed.

He was feeling foolish the next moment at seeing that Harbour had stiffened in pain, not in any readiness to reach out for him. And as the alarm went out of him he came back to the bunk again to ask, "Want some water?"

Jim was scarcely aware of what or who he was seeing as Talbot moved into his line of vision, for his brain was pounding with a skull-splitting ache. Each time he drew in a breath, pain lanced deep into his left side at the base of his ribs. He was never to know that Nye had kicked him, yet he was hazily remembering why his head hurt as Talbot spoke. The man's voice came only as a hollow and meaningless roar that added to the throbbing torment engulfing his senses.

Getting no response from Harbour, Talbot called, "Shep, he's coming to."

The big man, asleep on the adjoining bed, grunted, rolled over and shortly pushed himself up onto an elbow. He shook his head, then swung his feet to the floor and got up. By the time he stood beside Talbot, he was yawning and pulling on his shirt.

"He didn't seem to know I was talking to him."

"No? Then let's wake him up."

Jim winced as his hair was twisted, then

his head rocked around by a hard blow. The cabin's rough board ceiling spun before his eyes a moment, but the stinging of his face surprisingly enough let him regain his sense of balance so that the room stopped spinning.

A nausea hit him now and as he tried to keep from retching he turned onto his side, for the first time really seeing the two men alongside the bed. The shock of recognizing them, and of remembering that this was night and that he was at Crow Track, had a steadying effect on him so that when Talbot asked, "Want a drink?" he understood and weakly dipped his head in answer.

Talbot came back from the bucket by the door carrying a dipper. He was about to offer it to Jim when Nye reached out and took it from him. "Here's the way to give it to him, Harry."

Nye threw the dipper's contents squarely into Jim's face, guffawing as Jim flinched and gagged for breath. "Better go wake the boss, Harry."

"So you can knock Harbour out again? Hunh-uh. You go."

Jim listened dully to their brief wrangle but knew enough of what was being argued to be relieved when Nye finally left. The chill of the wetting he had taken and the coolness of the soaked blanket was beginning to clear his head and ease it of its ache, and when Talbot brought him a second dipperful of water he had the strength to push up to a sitting position and drink.

He noticed that the man stepped cautiously back out of his reach while he drank. Understanding the move and aware of how weak he was, Talbot's wariness suddenly struck him as being so absurd that he burst out laughing, surprised at hearing his voice as a hoarse and hollow booming.

Talbot gave him a wondering, worried look when he handed the dipper back. The effort of laughing had started his head pounding once more and to ease it he worked his legs around, lowered his boots to the boards and leaned over holding his head in his hands. His thoughts were still so disjointed that it took a deliberate effort to remember how he came to be here, to recall why he had come and to think back upon his talk with Renee and what had happened earlier in Alder.

Harry Talbot abruptly broke the long silence. "We thought you was out for good."

When Jim made no response, the Crow Track man spoke again. "You better be getting some answers thought up for Rue."

Jim tried to nod but only winced as another wave of pain stabbed his brain. When it began to ease, he asked thickly, "What time?"

"Going on five. Be light in another hour." Frowning in worry over Jim's slurred speech and his apparent weakness, Talbot asked, "You don't feel so good, huh?"

"I've felt —"

Jim checked his words at hearing boots crunching against the snow outside. The door abruptly swung open on Rue and Nye. Crow Track's owner came two strides into the room, glancing first at Jim, then questioningly to Talbot. Harry Talbot slowly shook his head and lifted a hand to tap his forehead, whereupon Rue eyed Jim with a blend of concern and irritation.

"Harry, you and Shep hang around outside."

Talbot had no liking for the prospect, yet the severe set of Rue's narrow face warned him against arguing. He stepped over to his bunk, got his coat and hat and went on out with Nye, shutting the door.

Rue pulled a straight-backed chair from the wall, placed it at the room's center and eased down onto it with arms folded across its back. "Just stay where you are and we'll get along fine, Harbour. Now what's this about Shep catching you making off with my rope?"

The man's appearance had served to clear Jim's brain. Except for the constant awareness of his head's dull aching and the soreness in his side, he found himself able to think rationally once more. He saw no point in answering Rue just yet and decided not to, hoping his silence would lead the man to believe that he was still groggy and didn't grasp what was being said.

"Hear you were up on the pass yesterday having a look-see." Rue's moustaches drooped in a wry expression. "Tonight we catch you here doing more of same. Where's it all getting you?"

When Jim still gave no sign of wanting to answer, even of having heard, Rue went on, "Think I know what you're trying for. You want to hang this Gardies killing on me because I was up there. Because I stood to gain most from getting rid of him. Well, you're wrong."

Jim lifted his head and stared dully across at the Crow Track man, who asked sharply, "You hear what I'm sayin'?"

Jim nodded weakly, trying to appear befuddled, too hurt and exhausted to speak. Rue frowned in annoyance now, saying, "You're wrong, hear? So wrong you won't believe it when I tell you."

"Tell . . . what?" Jim slurred his words intentionally, made his tone sound lifeless.

"That Ben Britt confessed tonight to killing Gardies. To killing him for some of the money he had on him."

Jim tried to hide his amazement at the man's bland admission of knowing about Britt's death. Yet his look must have betrayed his startlement, for Rue smiled meagerly and nodded. "That's gospel, Harbour. Bill Parks beat it out of him. More than that, Britt's dead."

On the point of pretending further ignorance, Jim checked himself, instead deciding to try and surprise the man by saying, "I know all that."

Sudden impassivity settled over Rue's features. "How do you know it?"

Jim let his head hang once more and ran a hand over his tender scalp, trying to think. He scarcely yet believed that Rue would this openly admit any knowledge whatsoever of what had happened earlier in Alder. He was all at once feeling keyed-up, his aching head and his sore side almost forgotten as Rue now echoed his question in a sharper tone. "How do you?"

Looking across the Crow Track man, and thinking carefully of what he was about to say, Jim drawled thickly, "I was there. Right after they locked Parks up."

Rue jerked straighter in the chair. "After what?" he asked incredulously.

Jim wanted to be very sure of where his

words were leading him and mumbled non-committally, "You heard."

"Get a grip on yourself, Harbour," Rue snapped. "Parks is locked up? Why?"

The man's hands were gripping the chair's back so tightly that his knuckles were white. Seeing the stiff middle finger of Rue's right hand pointing almost squarely at him, Jim was sharply reminded of the corrosive enmity this man bore him. Rue's present mood of mildness and reasoning would last only so long as he wanted it to, or as long as he was as unsure of himself as he now seemed to be.

Knowing that he had the barest chance of leaving Crow Track alive only if he prolonged this uncertainty in Rue, Jim now shook his head tiredly, muttering, "You were there. You ought to know."

"Not me," Rue was quick to say. He hesitated an instant before adding, "It was Fred Mayes that brought the word out. But he didn't know this about Parks. What happened?"

Once again Jim shook his head, trying to judge whether Rue was now lying or only confused. He was feeling a keen disappointment, the certainty that the man had been on the point of making a damaging admission slowly leaving him. "Don't ask me," he said apathetically. "The talk was that Parks didn't give such a straight story about Britt."

Rue was plainly alarmed and made no pretense at hiding his concern, probably thinking that Jim was too groggy to notice. He studied Jim covertly, as though trying to gauge how alert he was as he came up off the chair, asking, "Who locked him up?"

"Didn't hear."

The Crow Track owner stared vacantly at Jim a long moment, deliberating something that made him take out his watch and look at it, then glance briefly in the direction of the door. At length, thrusting hands in pockets and fixing Jim with a beetling stare, he said, "Let's forget about Parks and get down to cases. If you know Britt's dead, you know he owned up to killing Gardies. So what were you after here tonight?"

"The rope that threw Gardies' horse up on the pass."

Rue visibly stiffened at the impact of the words. For a moment he stood eyeing Jim warily. But abruptly his pale eyes took on a smug look. "All right. No reason why I shouldn't admit it now. It was my rope. Sure I stopped Gardies. Managed to knock him out. But I didn't kill him. Britt did."

What Hester Britt had told Wickwire made Jim believe he was hearing the truth. Yet he also realized that Phil Gardies would be alive now if it weren't for this man. And as he felt a stir of impotent fury, Rue blandly told him, "I'd do it again if I had it to do over."

"You would? Even without Neal?"

Rue's pretended puzzlement didn't quite mask his surprise. "What's Neal got to do with this?" he asked tonelessly.

"Neal's gone. Pulled out tonight. Left without his pay and in a hurry."

The Crow Track man shrugged. "Shep must've knocked your brains loose if you think I care a whit what's happened to Lew Neal. You aren't making sense."

His last words had been spoken almost absent-mindedly, as though his thoughts were on something else. The next moment Jim was sure of that as Rue swung abruptly to the door, opened it and called, "Shep, Harry."

The two Crow Track crewmen had barely entered the room before Rue was telling them, "Something's happened in town. I'm going in. You're to take turns watching our friend here." . . . He eyed Nye in much the same manner as he had earlier tonight . . . "Don't touch him unless he makes a break for it, Shep. And let him sleep if he wants. From the way he acts, you damn' near killed him."

"What d'you think he damn' near did to me yesterday?"

If Rue heard Nye's testy rejoinder he paid

it no attention, for he was studying Jim speculatively, coldly. And a moment later he drawled, "There's a long winter ahead. A man could drop out of sight without a prayer of anyone finding him till . . ."

He left the thought unfinished, either because he felt Jim wasn't listening or because he hadn't yet quite decided something. He buttoned his coat now, turned to the door and went out.

As the sound of his steps died away, Shep Nye walked across and pounded on the partition of the cook's room, bawling, "George, coffee. Hot and lots of it."

He kept on pounding the boards until the Chinaman gave a sleepy answer. Coming back to stand looking down at Jim, he asked, "Hear what the boss said? He's not through with you yet."

Jim lifted his head slowly and gave the man a dull, vacant look, whereupon Nye abruptly reached out, put a hand against his face and roughly shoved him back down on the bed, growling, "Sleep it off."

Jim lay motionless, convinced now that both Nye and Talbot must think he was still in possession of only half his wits. Thinking back on Rue's knowing about Britt's death, he was once again feeling let down, disappointed at the realization that Rue had apparently been here at the ranch when the killing took place.

He began thinking of his chances of getting out of here, and a full minute's consideration told him that those chances were very slender, practically nonexistent.

Nothing would please Nye more than another opportunity for working him over. Even Talbot would probably use a gun on him if forced to do it.

Only half-listening, he heard Harry Talbot ask Nye now, "Wonder how long it'll take Fred and Pierce's boys to get that herd across?"

"Day and a half. Two days."

"Glad Fred lost the toss. He can have sleepin' out this kind of weather."

Jim suddenly realized who they were talking about. And as he read a meaning into their words he turned his head, looked across at Talbot and asked, "Mayes is in Bend?"

Hearing him speak startled the man, put a questioning look in his eyes as he nodded and asked, "Feelin' better?"

"Some." Jim put a hand to his forehead and closed his eyes as though speaking was costing him a vast effort. Then, as casually as he could, he put another question. "Missed his turkey dinner did he?"

Talbot laughed dryly. "Not Fred. Probably

ate it at the hotel across there this noon."

Jim lay there with eyes closed, feeling the hard pound of his pulse. This was it. Fred Mayes hadn't brought the word of Britt's death to Crow Track tonight. He hadn't been within fifty miles of Alder. Rue had been lying.

Over the next ten minutes, Jim lay limply, pretending to be asleep. His thinking had gone on dead center, stopping at a point of certainty that Evan Rue was after all the man who had killed Britt. It didn't matter that he had only meager proof of this. His instinct told him that it must be fact.

He must have dozed off for a minute, for he wakened with a start as George brought in the coffee. Opening his eyes and turning his head, he looked across to see the Chinaman, pigtail hanging over shoulder, setting a big pot of coffee and three china mugs on the long table that ran across the room's inner end. He noticed idly that the faintest grey light of dawn was showing at the window behind Shep Nye.

George was on his way back into his room when Nye picked up the big graniteware pot and started filling the cups. He looked toward the bunk where Jim lay, calling, "Harbour, come and get it."

Talbot gave Nye a scowl and started reaching for one of the mugs. "Here, I'll take it to him."

Nye reached out and caught his hand, a down-lipped smile twisting his scarred and swollen face. "Let him get it."

"Supposin' he can't even walk?"

"Then he doesn't get any." As Talbot turned away with a look of disgust, Nye glanced Jim's way once again, seeing that his eyes were open. "On your feet, tall man."

Jim pushed up slowly, slid his boots off the edge of the bed and sat a long moment with head lowered, as though feeling dizzy, weak. Then he tried to stand.

He was weaker than he had realized and it took no great pretense to sit suddenly back down on the bed again. He shook his head, whereupon Nye chuckled, asking, "Going to make it?"

"Hell, Shep. Take it over to him."

"If he can't walk, he can crawl," Nye drawled. "Come along, Harbour. Try again."

Jim did, this time placing his boots wider apart so as to keep his balance. After a brief moment in which the room tilted before his eyes, he felt his strength coming back. He started toward the table in a slow, spraddle-legged stride. Halfway to it he stopped, lifted hands to face and stood for long seconds. Then when he started on again he intentionally let one knee buckle and fell awkwardly sideways to the floor.

Harry Talbot started toward him but was stopped by Nye's, "Let him be." Then the big man watched Jim come to his knees and erect once more.

Nye still stood with his back to the window at the end of the table where the coffee steamed in the three mugs. He reached over now, handed one mug to Talbot, took one himself and nodded down to the other as Jim started toward him.

Jim was two strides short of the man and lifting a hand as though reaching out to steady himself by a hold on the table when he suddenly lunged. His legs felt loose, weak as he put all the drive of his high frame into slamming shoulder-first into Nye.

There was an instant when he felt Nye's heavy bulk stay rock solid. But then the man fell backward into the window. Nye cried out hoarsely as his back slammed into the glass and smashed it. Jim felt himself falling outward as Nye's coffee splashed across his shirt. Then the Crow Track man was falling out from under him, he felt the hard chill of the night air and an instant later drove the breath out of Nye as he fell onto him and rolled over in the snow.

Nye shouted, "Harry," as Jim rolled clear and came to his feet running. Jim lost his balance, fell hard against the wall, managed to keep his footing, and a moment later dove around the kitchen end of the cabin.

A gun laid its deafening thunder across the near-darkness from the cabin's front. Jim dodged hard aside at seeing the shape of the well house suddenly loom before him. A second hard explosion, a louder one, reached out at him. Somewhere behind him Nye bellowed unintelligibly. He swung to his right now, toward the corral, hearing the fast pound of boots sounding from the direction of the cabin. He was beginning to reach for breath as he ran past the corral and toward the trees.

A hard blow along the outside of his right thigh marked the exact instant a gun's thunder blasted out behind him once more. He lunged to his left, then back to his right as he came abreast the first tall lodgepole and ran into deeper snow. Something he had failed to see in the weak light tripped him and he dove headlong into a drift. He struggled to his feet and started running again, slowly now.

"Over there, Harry. Off to your left," he heard Nye bawling.

He came across the deep imprints his boots had made in coming out of the trees hours ago and thankfulness rose in him as he jogged along following them. He was gagging for breath, feeling the drive going from his legs when he finally stumbled up to the mare and jerked the reins loose from a tree's branch. He lifted a boot to stirrup and somehow managed to pull himself into the saddle.

One more bullet came his way as he kicked the mare into a labored run. The branch it sheared from a tree close by struck him on the cheek. Then he was away.

Thirty-five minutes later, as the sky behind the Arrowheads was brightening with a strong orange light, Tom Murchison rode up to the big house at Bit to find Renee up, to tell her that Jim Harbour had just ridden out the town road on a fresh horse.

"Wouldn't say where he'd been or where he was going," Murchison told her. "He asked for the loan of a colt and my forty-five. There was blood along his leg but he wouldn't let me look at it. Said it was only a scratch. Where's he been?"

"I'm almost afraid to know." Renee was pale from a sleepless night and her voice held a hollow ring as she said, "Tom, run as fast as you can and bring me the sorrel."

"I guessed you'd be wantin' him. So I brought him along."

"Bless you, Tom." She turned and ran quickly to her room.

* * *

Rue had been in a hurry when he left Crow Track but had soon decided that there was no need for such haste. So he was holding the grey to an easy jog as he rode into the foot of Alder's main street. Coming up on the Britt house he eyed it with a faint smile, wondering what had panicked him back there at the ranch. Harbour could have been wrong. Or, if he was right, some simple explanation lay behind Bill Parks' difficulties.

He intended finding out what, if any, these difficulties were. And as he debated how to proceed with that, how to set about it without seeming to be unduly curious, he decided he would first go to the hotel for coffee, as would any other rider arriving in town this early in the day.

The squeal of the grey's hooves against the crusty snow and the rhythmic creaking of leather were the only sounds that reached him this bitter cold, still morning. They were sounds that threatened to lull him to overconfidence so that at one interval he had to tell himself, *If he's locked in his jail, something's gone wrong,* to believe that this wasn't just another peaceful, quiet winter morning.

Up ahead he saw Judge Bullock sweeping his brick walk, and he touched the grey with spur, swinging in off the street shortly to call,

"You're at it early, Judge," as he reined in.

"Morning, Rue." Bullock's manner wasn't overly friendly.

"Hear you had some excitement in here last night." Rue spoke loudly, remembering the man's deafness.

"Terrible thing," the judge sighed, "But when a man takes to drink, such things happen. Ben's better off in the grave. So's Hester better off for having him there."

Rue nodded sagely, thinking it odd that old Bullock hadn't mentioned whatever trouble the sheriff was involved in. He decided then to fish more directly for the information he sought. "Good job Bill Parks did."

"Yes, sir. Parks has the makings of a fine peace officer." The judge resumed his sweeping then, adding, "So cold this morning a man's got to keep moving."

Frowning, more puzzled at each passing moment, Rue now asked, "Wonder where I'd find Parks this time of morning."

Bullock's look was startled. "It's a little early in the day for me to answer that. I'd start at the hotel. It's about breakfast time."

"Guess I will."

Going on up the street, Rue didn't know what to think. Certainly Bullock should know if anything as drastic as Harbour spoke of had happened to Parks. He was confused and worried as he presently came down out of the saddle and tied at the hotel rail.

He went in to the clerk behind the desk at the foot of the lobby stairway, asking as casually as he could, "The sheriff come down from his room yet?"

"Let's see." The man yawned, having only minutes ago come to work. He glanced around at the board of keys behind him. "Key's here. Guess he must've beat me up."

Rue walked on over and peered into the dining room, which was empty. Once again he was confounded by a man who should have known, knowing nothing of Bill Parks being in trouble.

He was impatient now and decided he wouldn't be risking much if he went straight to the courthouse. He was empty, wanting a meal and feeling the cold as he shortly went on down the street. Stepping into the courthouse's gloomy hallway, its stale air at once reminded him of what had gone on here last night. As he opened the door to the sheriff's office he was imagining he could still smell a faint trace of gunpowder in the air.

The office was empty, pitch dark, the blind at the window still drawn. He stepped on over and raised it, seeing at once that the jail door was padlocked. He felt a chill run along his spine as he stepped over there, hit the door with his fist and called, "Bill."

He had no answer. He beat the heavy door several more times, calling more loudly, "Bill, wake up."

Suddenly he heard a muffled voice. He shouted, "That you, Bill?"

Once again there was an answer, indistinguishable except for the querulous tone of a voice that could belong to no one but Bill Parks.

"Hold on." Rue turned and looked about the office for something with which to pry off the door's heavy hasp. He found nothing, thought of his .38, of blowing the padlock apart. But common sense cautioned him against this, against rousing anyone's curiosity over what he was about to do. He even wondered if someone on the street might possibly have heard his shouting now as he went out into the hallway, suddenly having remembered something.

At the back end of the hall was a row of half a dozen red-painted fire buckets filled with sand. Above them hung a double-bitted axe. Rue lifted the axe down, hurried back into the office and closed the door.

He went to the window, glancing both ways along the street, seeing no one on this walk or on the one opposite. Crossing the room, he spread his boots wide and swung the axe.

Long years of chopping and splitting wood made his first hard stroke a telling one. The axe bit deep into the wood close above the hasp, shearing one bolt. At his second vicious swing the hasp and padlock jumped free.

Rue pulled the door back, stepped into the darkened jail. A moment later Bill Parks said complainingly, relievedly, "Time you got here."

"Could have made it earlier if you'd let me know. What's —"

"Let you know?" The sheriff's tone was petulant. "How the devil could I? They weren't that accommodating."

"Who's 'they,' Bill?"

"Harbour and Wickwire, who else?" Parks struck a match now and reached up to light a lantern hanging from a wire fastened to the cell's ceiling.

A hard apprehension was gripping Rue. "Only those two?"

"Only those two." The stump of the law man's bad arm lifted, fell. "They gave me a bad time for a few minutes there. How'd you hear about it? The last I knew Harbour said he was on his way out to bring you . . ."

His words broke off as Rue savagely motioned him to silence. For Rue was thinking back now, remembering the rope, remembering other things.

"How much do they know, Bill?"

"Nothing for sure. So far it's only guesses. But that Harbour, he's beginning to add things up."

"Such as?"

"Doc Emery heard you ride out the alley last night, first of all. Then they found the back door unbolted. I —"

Rue swore in a clipped, brittle voice. "You didn't lock it after me?"

"And run the chance of someone walkin' in on me doing it? Hell, no, I didn't. I'd barely followed you on out and got onto the walk when Red Simpson came along." He nodded to the lock on the cell door. "Get me out of here."

Breathing a baffled, angry sigh, Rue looked at the lock. "How, without a key?"

"The same way you busted in."

"The axe hasn't been made that would break open that iron. Besides, it'd make so much noise we'd have the whole town in."

Parks' glance narrowed. "If you think —"

"Don't worry, I'll get you out." Rue's thinking was coming fast and clear now. "What else do they know?"

"Seems Ben told Hester when I went to get him that he'd shot Gardies by accident. Told her what he told us, I reckon."

Rue considered that, scowling darkly.

"Who's going to believe anything Ben told her? If she gets that story around, all you have to say is he must've guessed what was coming and was trying to cook up a story to cover what he'd done."

"But Harbour and that card sharp think he told her the truth."

"Let 'em." Rue eyed his friend coldly for a moment. "The only chance we're taking is with you, Bill."

Parks straightened, hefted his belt higher on his sloping paunch with a quick jerk. "Meaning what?"

"You're so damn scared right now you're liable to blab if those two come at you another time."

The law man clenched his fist. A slow change eased the anger from his loose face, replacing it with a smug, purposeful look. "Things've switched around some since last night, since you put that hole through Ben, Ev. You don't crack the whip any more the way you been doing."

They eyed each other coolly, the law man not flinching, Rue sizing him up with an understanding that he no longer held the hole card in their relations. He accepted that fact calmly, and his tone had lost its rough edge when he next spoke. "We'll make out all right, Bill. But only if we use our noodles. Now sit yourself down and wait'll I get back."

He was turning away when Parks asked, "Where you going?"

"After a crow bar, anything that'll let me pry you out of there."

The sheriff's eyes showed an instant concern. "What if Wickwire sees you wandering around here?"

Rue pulled his coat aside and ran his hand along the scuffed leather of his holster. Seeing that, Parks said, "The coat makes it hard to get at."

"Then I'll carry it this way." The Crow Track man lifted the Smith and Wesson from holster, dropped it into the right-hand pocket of his coat, then turned on out into the office.

George Wickwire had spent a restless night, waking time after time to wonder about Jim and to blame himself for not having ridden out to Bit and Crow Track with his friend.

He was wide awake at five o'clock but lay in bed another hour, until the sun was burning away the light overcast. He took his time shaving and dressing, thinking mostly of Hester Britt now and planning how they were to expand the stage line by buying freight wagons and probably two new coaches.

Tying his string tie, he sauntered over to the street-facing window and looked out, seeing the store roofs powdered with a light fall of new snow. The slow and steady thud of an axe sounded from up the street. Across the way two men turned into the restaurant.

Looking idly below, he saw a lone animal at the rail beyond the wide walk. He was turning away from the window when suddenly he gave a start of surprise, glanced down again. He made out the Crow Track brand on the grey's shoulder.

He whistled softly, then hurried to strap on the shoulder-holster and pull on his coat. The fur-collared overcoat across his arm, he took the stairs into the lobby two steps at a time, turning to the counter at the bottom to ask the clerk, "Rue been in, Max?"

The man nodded. "Ten minutes ago."

"Where is he now?"

"Couldn't tell you. He was asking for Parks. Then he went on out."

Wickwire shrugged into the heavy coat on his way across the dingy lobby. He stopped short of the door of the glassed-in veranda and looked up the street, then down. He saw three men on the walks, one across the way, two coming from the direction of the *Niagara*, none of whom was Rue. He went on out and was slowly descending the steps to the walk when he heard the cadenced beat of a pony's hooves sounding from far down the street.

In another quarter-minute he saw that the approaching rider was Jim Harbour. The fact that Jim was hatless blended a strong apprehension with his feeling of relief. He waited there on the walk as Jim angled in off the street toward the rail, toward Rue's grey.

Jim reined in, looking at the grey, then at Wickwire with a silent question in his eyes. The gambler nodded. "He's here somewhere. Haven't located him yet."

Coming down out of the saddle, then tying his Bit horse, Jim joined his friend on the walk. Wickwire noticed that he was limping, noticed his paleness and the lines of tiredness about his eyes. "So you got to him?"

Jim nodded.

"How many of them worked you over?" The gambler glanced down at Jim's leg. "Why're you lame?"

"Stubbed my toe." Jim smiled sparely as his restless glance roved the street.

"Going to tell me about it?"

There was a shadow of concern in Jim's eyes as he briefly told his friend about Rue's rope and about the man's lie of having heard of the Britt killing from one of his crew.

Wickwire's face took on a chill and piercing gravity as he listened. "So where to now?" he asked as Jim finished.

"We could have a look at the jail." Jim was

looking down the street, the concern still in his eyes. "Someone was behind me on the way in, gaining on me all the way. We'd better get at this." And he started down the walk toward the courthouse.

They were two buildings beyond the hotel when they heard that other rider coming up the street at a run. Jim slowed his stride. "If it's Nye or one of those others, you keep him busy, George. I'm going after Rue."

Wickwire didn't speak at once, for the rider down there this moment came into sight from behind the trees far down Main Street. Then in another moment he was saying, "No trouble here. See who it is."

Jim recognized Renee with a momentary lift of excitement. But then a sharp regret, almost an annoyance, settled through him as Wickwire said, "We'd better wait right here."

They stopped, and in another few seconds Renee saw them and turned her animal obliquely toward them out of the street's center. Her sorrel was badly blown, his mouth foam-flecked and his flanks steaming as she pulled him to a halt beyond the near rail.

For a moment her glance clung to Jim, betraying a blend of outright relief and gladness. "I was afraid I might be too late. Tom said you looked . . ."

She didn't finish what she had been about to say, and shortly Jim told her, "We're on our way to see how the sheriff likes his accommodations, Renee." He was noticing her high-strung and near-exhausted look and added, "If you'll go to the hotel, we'll be with you in —"

A sound off to his left, further along the walk, made him check his words and glance quickly that way. What he saw was Evan Rue stepping from the narrow passageway at the corner of the building beyond, some thirty feet away.

The man was carrying a length of pipe perhaps three feet long. And now as he strode onto the walk, his glance, which had been directed down the street, swung around to them.

His surprise turned his narrow face instantly slack. He halted sharply, coming more erect and turning slowly this way. Jim noticed that his right hand, the one with the bullet-stiffened middle finger, was in the pocket of his coat.

Rue's glance abruptly fell away. He reached back deliberately to lean the length of pipe against the nearby wall of the hardware store. Facing them once more, he said, "Didn't expect to see you here, Harbour."

Jim was hard aware of Renee stepping down out of the saddle now as he drawled, "Rue, you got your story crossed. They tell me Fred Mayes has been over in Bend since yesterday noon."

The Crow Track man arched his brows in what looked like surprise, his left hand lifting slowly to stroke his tobacco-yellow moustaches. "So he has. Did I say it was Fred? My mistake. I meant Mose."

"No, Rue," Wickwire inserted quietly. "You meant yourself."

Jim had the barest fraction of a second's warning of what was coming. For Rue's chill, pale eyes seemed to veil over now. He saw the man's pocket bulge suddenly with an object larger than a hand. And as he slashed his coat aside he lunged hard against Wickwire.

The pounding explosion of Rue's .38 ripped away the momentary silence the instant Jim felt a light tap along the top of his right shoulder. Then he was arcing Tom Murchison's worn .45 Colt's up and clear of leather, thumbing back its stiff hammer as he lifted it into line.

He had a split-second's clear image of Rue's hate-contorted face as the man tried to draw his weapon from the smoking pocket of his coat. Then he squeezed trigger, the .38's second blast prolonging the sound of his own shot.

Rue was jarred backward. A strong surprise,

a wonder, briefly shadowed his long face before a vacant look washed all expression from his pale eyes. And Jim was letting the Colt's drop to his side as the man's knees buckled and he went down.

George Wickwire let his breath go sharply, checking his convulsive reach under coat to the weapon at his shoulder. He looked around at Jim in awe to ask, "Just how did that thing come to be in your hand?"

Jim made no answer, for his glance had gone to Renee to find her standing frozen in terror, her face a chalky white as she stared at him.

The motion he made of holstering the Colt's seemed to stir her from her paralysis, for now she came slowly across and up onto the walk to within a stride of him. She gave Rue's body a fleeting, horrified look that made Jim tell her gently, "It's over, Renee. It had to be done."

"I know, I know," she breathed. "But it . . . at first I thought I was losing you."

Suddenly her eyes were alight with warmth. Behind that lay a thankfulness, a yearning he found hard to believe.

Somewhere opposite a door slammed. And as three men ran this way from the restaurant across there, George Wickwire started toward Rue's body, quickly saying, "You two could wait at the hotel while I tidy this up."

Jim took Renee's arm, turning her up the walk. She tightened her arm against his touch, looking up at him in humility and wonderment. "I'm just now realizing how wrong it was asking you to help, Jim. If it had been you, not him . . ."

He felt her trembling and said, "I was doing it for myself. And you did have the right to ask it."

She shook her head, glancing down at the walk as the shock of what she had seen slowly left her. Neither of them spoke then until they were coming in on the hotel steps, until she murmured, "Now you'll be going back up into the hills."

This past minute had brought him a realization so unsettling that he found it hard to think, to tell himself, *She doesn't even have Neal any more.*

"No hurry for that," he said.

"You mean it, Jim? You'll stay?"

"Until the outfit's squared away and running as it should."

The gladness in her eyes made a certainty of a new awareness that had only seconds ago come to him. And as he tried to look out across the days that were to come he could scarcely take in their promise.

Peter Dawson is the *nom de plume* used by Jonathan Hurff Glidden for all of his fiction. It was also used once by Frederick Faust, better known as Max Brand, for a magazine story, and by Otis Gaylord for a series of eight novels. The name itself is derived from a popular brand of Scotch whiskey. Glidden was born in Kewanee, Illinois, and was graduated from the University of Illinois with a degree in English literature. He came first to write Western fiction because of prompting from his brother Frederick Dilley Glidden who wrote Western fiction under the pseudonym Luke Short. In his career as a Western writer, he has written sixteen Western novels and over 120 Western novelettes and short stories for the magazine market. Glidden from the beginning was a dedicated craftsman who revised and polished his fiction until it shone as a fine gem. His Peter Dawson novels are noted for their adept plotting, interesting and well developed characters, their authentically researched historical backgrounds, and his stylistic flair. His first novel THE CRIMSON HORSESHOE won the Dodd, Mead Prize as the best Western of the year 1941 and ran serially in Street and Smith's WESTERN STORY

MAGAZINE prior to book publication. During the Second World War, Glidden served with the U.S. Strategic and Tactical Air Force in the United Kingdom. Later in 1950 he served for a time as Assistant to Chief of Station in Germany. After the war, his novels were frequently serialized in THE SATURDAY EVENING POST. In paperback, his books have already sold 25,000,000 copies worldwide and have been translated into numerous foreign languages. Dawson titles such as HIGH COUNTRY, GUNSMOKE GRAZE, and ROYAL GORGE are generally conceded to be among his masterpieces although he was an extremely consistent writer and virtually all his fiction has retained its classic stature among readers of all generations. His short story "Long Gone" (1950) was adapted for the screen as FACE OF A FUGITIVE (Columbia, 1959) starring Fred MacMurray and James Coburn. His earlier classic Western novels are being reprinted in hardcover by Chivers, Ltd., for the English-reading world and many of his longer novel-length titles, beginning with RATTLESNAKE MESA, are appearing for the first time in book form.

The employees of THORNDIKE PRESS hope you have enjoyed this Large Print book. All our Large Print books are designed for easy reading — and they're made to last.

Other Thorndike Large Print books are available at your library, through selected bookstores, or directly from us. Suggestions for books you would like to see in Large Print are always welcome.

For more information about current and upcoming titles, please call or mail your name and address to:

THORNDIKE PRESS
PO Box 159
Thorndike, Maine 04986
800/223-6121
207/948-2962